D0777692
Betty and Veronica®
DECADES
The 1960s

Written by

Frank Doyle, George Gladir, Jim Ruth, & Dick Malmgren

Art by

Dan DeCarlo, Rudy Lapick, Vince DeCarlo,
Bill Vigoda, & Victor Gorelick

Publisher / Co-CEO: Jon Goldwater
President / Editor-In-Chief: Mike Pellerito
Chief Creative Officer: Roberto Aguirre-Sacasa
Chief Operating Officer: William Mooar
Chief Financial Officer: Robert Wintle
Director: Jonathan Betancourt
Senior Director of Editorial: Jamie Lee Rotante
Production Manager: Stephen Oswald
Art Director: Vincent Lovallo
Director of Publicity & Social Media: Ron Cacace
Lead Designer: Kari McLachlan
Associate Editor: Carlos Antunes
Co-CEO: Nancy Silberkleit

Printed in Canada. First Printing. ISBN: 978-1-64576-911-8

Introduction by DAN PARENT

When you look at the rich history of Archie Comics, there are so many areas to explore. From the momentous beginnings in 1941, to the explosion on the small screen with *Riverdale* in 2017, there have been decades of comics and thousands of stories published. And in my opinion, the pinnacle of these stories revolve around Dan DeCarlo in the 1960s!

This was the decade when the Dan DeCarlo style became THE Archie Comics house style. His pages were a combination of comic art and VOGUE and GLAMOUR magazines. His illustrations of the girls jump off the page, and he became to Archie what John Romita was to Marvel and Neal Adams was to DC. He was the master!

The decade was also incredible for Betty and Veronica (and Archie Comics overall), since the 1960s was a time capsule of progression and change, which also translated into the stories. The trends and styles of the decade were prominently featured in these stories. *Betty and Veronica* was such a popular title, it sold almost as well as the main *Archie* title, and kept that position for years.

And as great as ALL the writers and artists were in this incredible decade, there was one formula for the perfect Archie story. It's one part Betty and Veronica, one part Frank Doyle, and one part Dan DeCarlo. It doesn't get better than that!

__DAN PARENT__ is a fan-favorite writer and artist who has worked at Archie Comics for over 30 years. He started his art career at Archie working alongside the legendary Dan DeCarlo.

This book contains some material that was originally created in a less socially sensitive time in our society and reflects attitudes that may be interpreted as being unacceptable today. The stories are reprinted here without alteration for historical reference.

Betty and Veronica®
DECADES

Script: Frank Doyle / Art: Dan DeCarlo

Originally printed in ARCHIE'S GIRLS BETTY & VERONICA #52, APRIL 1960

NO BOY IS GOING TO TREAT ME THAT WAY AND GET AWAY WITH IT!
I'LL SHOW HIM THAT HE CAN'T TRIFLE WITH MY AFFECTIONS!!
WELL, I'LL BOW OUT BEFORE THE FIREWORKS!
'BYE, DEAR!
SMITHERS!!
YES, MISS VERONICA?
IF THAT ARCHIE CHARACTER SHOWS UP, THROW HIM OUT!
THERE'S NOT MUCH CHANCE OF THAT MISS VERONICA!
I HEARD YOUR SPAT LAST WEEK!
HE'LL NEVER SHOW HIS FACE AROUND HERE AGAIN!
IS THAT SO?
I'LL GET HIM OVER HERE IF I HAVE TO BEG ON BENDED KNEE! - AND THEN YOU CAN THROW HIM OUT!

ARCHIE? THIS IS VERONICA!
RONNIE! - BABY! - LOVER-DOLL! CAN YOU EVER FORGIVE ME? I'VE BEEN A BEAST!
W-WELL! I- ER - THAT IS. - I ---
PLEASE, BABY!
I CAN'T BEAR BEING AWAY FROM YOU, SUGAR-PLUM!
PLEASE TAKE ME BACK!!
(SNIFF) W-WHY, ARCHIEKINS! OF C-COURSE I FORGIVE YOU!!
H-HURRY OVER! W-WE'VE WASTED S-SO MUCH TIME!!
EEYAHOO!!
HE DIDN'T FORGET ME! HE STILL LOVES ME!!
OOOH! I'M SO HAPPY!!

DARLING! I'M HERE!
WHAM!
SWEETHEART!! HOW NICE OF YOU TO LEAVE THE DOOR OPEN!
HEY!!
ORDERS, SONNY! NOTHING PERSONAL!
I'VE BEEN SO MISERABLE WITHOUT MY ARCHIE!
I'LL NEVER FIGHT WITH THE DEAR BOY AGAIN!
SMITHERS! I'M EXPECTING ARCHIE AT ANY MOMENT!
NOW STOP WORRYING, MISS VERONICA! I TOOK CARE OF THAT ONE!
YOK, YOK! YOU SHOULD HAVE SEEN HIM BOUNCE!
(GASP!) H-HE'S BEEN HERE?

AND-AND YOU THREW HIM OUT!
ISN'T THAT W-WHAT YOU WANTED?
WAH! NOW HE'LL NEVER COME BACK!! YOU'VE RUINED EVERYTHING!!
EGAD!!
I'LL GET HIM, IF I HAVE TO DRAG HIM BACK BY THE SCRUFF OF HIS NECK!
YIPE! HE'S STILL AFTER ME!
COME BACK, MASTER ARCHIE! COME BACK!
HE'S S-SLOW, BUT, BOY, IS HE PERSISTENT!
RONNIE'S HOUSE! HE'LL NEVER THINK OF LOOKING FOR ME THERE!
LODGE

ARCHIEKINS! LOVER-BOY! YOU'VE COME BACK TO ME.!!
THAT SWALLOW-TAILED SHEEP DOG OF YOURS HERDED ME IN HERE LIKE A STRAY LAMB!
(PUFF, PUFF) IT'S NO U-USE, MISS VERONICA! I C-CAN'T CATCH ---
--ULP!!
SMACK!
SMITHERS! YOU LOVABLE, OVERWEIGHT CUPID, YOU!
YOU DID IT! I'LL SEE TO IT THAT DADDY RAISES YOUR SALARY!
SOMEHOW, IN ALL THAT CONFUSION, I DID THE RIGHT THING!
I WONDER WHAT IT WAS?
THE END

Script: Frank Doyle / Art: Dan DeCarlo

Originally printed in ARCHIE'S GIRLS BETTY & VERONICA #53, MAY 1960

YOU SEE, MY FRIENDS ARE ON ONE SIDE OF THE FENCE, --- MY ENEMIES ON THE OTHER!
--AND VERONICA?
SHE'S SITTING RIGHT ON THAT FENCE!
UNDERSTAND, JUGGIE! I LOVE RONNIE!
SHE'S TRULY MY FRIEND! SHE'S MY VERY BEST FRIEND!
WHY, WE HAVE EVERYTHING IN COMMON!
DOES THAT INCLUDE ARCHIE?
THAT'S WHERE THE ENEMY PART COMES IN!

IT'S A SIMPLE MATTER OF DEGREE!
EXPLAIN!
ALL YOU HAVE TO DO IS FIND OUT IF SHE IS MORE FRIEND THAN ENEMY!
THAT'S ALL, EH?
IF YOU LIKE HER MORE THAN YOU HATE HER, CUT OUT ARCHIE!
IF YOU HATE HER MORE, STOP BEING FRIENDLY WITH HER!
OH, YOU AND YOUR OLD LOGIC!
ALRIGHT, I'LL LEAVE IT UP TO HER!
SHE'LL EITHER MAKE ME LIKE HER, ---
---OR HATE HER!

BETTY, DARLING! YOU'RE JUST THE GIRL I'VE BEEN WANTING TO SEE!
WILL YOU PLEASE TAKE MY BLACK FORMAL OFF MY HANDS? I MUST GET RID OF IT!
B-BUT IT'S BRAND NEW!
I'VE SEEN ONE I LIKE BETTER!
DAD WON'T LET ME BUY ANOTHER ONE IF I STILL HAVE THIS ONE!
SEE? SEE HOW HARD SHE'S TRYING TO BE FRIENDLY!
DARLING, YOU'VE GOT TO TAKE IT! IT WILL LOOK DIVINE ON YOU!
OF COURSE I'LL TAKE IT, RON! I'M MAD ABOUT THIS GOWN!
BUT YOU SURE MAKE IT HARD FOR A GIRL TO COME TO A DECISION!
HUH? WHAT DECISION?

VERONICA! BETTY! I HAVE SOMETHING FOR YOU TWO GIRLS!
OH! HELLO, MR. LODGE!
HERE YOU ARE! TWO TICKETS TO THE HORSE SHOW NEXT SATURDAY AFTERNOON!
GOLLEE!
OOH! DADDY! YOU'RE AN ANGEL!
GOSH! THANKS, MR. LODGE!
NOW WATCH! WATCH CLOSELY! HERE IT COMES!
SHE'LL FIGURE OUT SOME WAY TO SQUEEZE ME OUT SO THAT SHE CAN GO WITH ARCHIE!
DON'T MISS THIS, NOW!
OMIGOSH! NEXT SATURDAY AFTERNOON! GOLLY! I'M SORRY, BETTY!
SEE? SEE?

WE, -ER-CAN'T GO TOGETHER, EH?
I'M AFRAID NOT, DARLING!
I HAVE AN APPOINTMENT FOR A PERMANENT THAT DAY!
WELL, AT LEAST I KNOW WHICH SIDE OF THE FENCE TO PUT----
--- Y-YOU CAN'T GO?
NO!
BUT WE NEEDN'T WASTE THE TICKET! WHY DON'T YOU TAKE ARCHIE?
VERONICA LODGE, YOU SPOILED EVERYTHING!!
SHE WAS SUPPOSED TO TAKE ARCHIE, AND THEN I COULD HATE HER, AND THEN---
OH, WHAT'S THE USE!
IT WOULD HAVE BEEN A REAL GOOD STORY IF SHE HADN'T SPOILED IT WITH HER DARNED OLD GENEROSITY!
THE END

Script: Frank Doyle / Pencils: Dan DeCarlo / Inks: Rudy Lapick / Letters: Vince DeCarlo

Originally printed in ARCHIE'S GIRLS BETTY & VERONICA #54, JUNE 1960

BUT, MISS GRUNDY! I DIDN'T DO ANYTHING!
A GIRL LIKE YOU DOESN'T HAVE TO DO ANYTHING TO CAUSE TROUBLE!
YOU DON'T SEE BETTY CLUTTERING UP THE HALLS WITH BOYS!
WHY CAN'T YOU BE MORE LIKE HER?
SHE NEVER CAUSES ANY TROUBLE!
DO YOU, BETTY?
NO, MISS GRUNDY! THAT'S THE TROUBLE!
--HUH?
(SIGH) N-NEVER MIND, MISS GRUNDY!

ALL RIGHT, CLASS! NOW, TODAY WE ARE GOING TO DELVE INTO THE -----
ICA
---ARCHIE! REGGIE! WILL YOU PLEASE PAY ATTENTION!!
VERONICA! SUPPOSE YOU SIT OVER HERE!
TAP! TAP!
YOU MAKE LIFE DIFFICULT FOR US TEACHERS!
WHY CAN'T YOU BE MORE LIKE YOUR FRIEND, BETTY?
YOU'LL NOTICE THAT SHE DOESN'T KEEP THE BOYS FROM PAYING ATTENTION TO THEIR STUDIES!!
R
HMPH! BIG DEAL! TEACHER'S PET!

WAP!
EEP!
ZOOM
STOP! HALT! DON'T MOVE.!!
BETTY! YOU MAY GO!
I'LL SEE YOU TWO AFTER SCHOOL! IN MY OFFICE!
PERHAPS YOU HAD BETTER BE THERE TOO!
AFTER ALL, YOU WERE THE CAUSE OF THAT REVOLTING DISPLAY OF BAD MANNERS!

HEY! THE KIDS GOT THEMSELVES IN TROUBLE, EH?
THEY KNOCKED POOR MR. WEATHERBEE DOWN IN THEIR HURRY TO GET TO RONNIE!
HEE, HEE! THAT GIRL IS LIKE THE FUSE IN A STICK OF DYNAMITE!
NUTS! YOU CAN'T BLAME THEIR TROUBLE ON HER!
WHO CAN'T? SHE'S A BORN TROUBLE MAKER!
YOU'RE OUT OF YOUR MIND!
IT WASN'T HER FAULT!
IT'S ALWAYS HER FAULT!
IT IS NOT!
IT IS!
NOT!
IS!

HERE, HERE! STOP THIS INSTANT! BREAK THIS UP!!
BETTY COOPER, I'M ASHAMED OF YOU! COME ALONG WITH ME!
---INCITING A RIOT!
DISRUPTING THE SCHOOL! CAUSING A COMMOTION IN THE HALLS!
--BOYS FIGHTING OVER HER!
INDEED?
BETTY COOPER! WHAT HAVE YOU GOT TO SAY TO THESE CHARGES?
(SIGH) J-JUST, --THANKS, MISS GRUNDY! YOU'VE MADE ME THE HAPPIEST GIRL IN SCHOOL!
?
THE END

Script: Frank Doyle / Pencils: Dan DeCarlo / Inks: Rudy Lapick / Letters: Vince DeCarlo

Originally printed in ARCHIE'S GIRLS BETTY & VERONICA #54, JUNE 1960

OH! HA, HA! YOU'RE KIDDING ME! YOU THOUGHT IT LOOKED LIKE ARCHIE, TOO!
IT WAS ARCHIE!
BUT DON'T WORRY! THAT WAS ONLY HIS COUSIN, SALLY!
"C-COUSIN?"
SHE COMES FROM FLORIDA!
COUSIN, EH?
SHE'S JUST HERE FOR A SHORT VISIT!
SURE SHE IS!
NATURALLY, HIS MOTHER INSISTS THAT HE ENTERTAIN HER!
OH, NATURALLY! AND WHERE DOES THIS MOUNTAIN OF INFORMATION COME FROM?
FROM ARCHIE, OF COURSE!
--- AND YOU SWALLOW THIS, --ER-YOU BELIEVE HIM?
I TRUST MY ARCHIEKINS!

I DON'T KNOW ABOUT YOU FOLKS, BUT I'M,-ER- LIKE SKEPTICAL!
HEY, YOU'RE NOT SUPPOSED TO TALK TO THOSE PEOPLE OUT THERE!
OH, FIDDLE, FADDLE!
I'M THE FRIENDLY TYPE!
I LIKE TO TALK TO THE READERS!
SO ANYWAY, WHAT WAS IT ALL ABOUT?
ARCHIE JUST PASSED WITH A GORGEOUS CHICK THAT HE'S PASSING OFF AS HIS COUSIN!
YIP! HE'S IN FOR A RUMBLE WITH RONNIE IF SHE GETS THE WORD!
THAT'S JUST IT!
SHE CAUGHT THE WHOLE SCENE AND DIDN'T SO MUCH AS ELEVATE AN EYEBROW!
YUK! YUK!

YOK, YOK! THAT'S REAL FRANTIC! NOW WHAT'S THE PUNCH LINE?
MY WORD AS A RED-BLOODED, GIRL SCOUT TYPE AMERICAN!
VERONICA TRUSTS ARCHIE!
THAT'S A FUNNY PUNCH LINE ALL RIGHT! WHO'S YOUR WRITER?
HMPH!
SAY, LOOK! YOU SAW THE WHOLE THING! DID IT REALLY HAPPEN LIKE SHE SAID?
---IT DID?
MAN! LIKE I'VE GOT TO GET THIS STRAIGHT FROM THE MARE'S OWN MOUTH!
LEVEL WITH ME, RON! DID YOU REALLY SEE ARCHIE WITH A BEAUTIFUL CHICK?
WHY, YES, JUGGIE!

--- AND THIS DOLL-TYPE IS SUPPOSED TO BE A RELATIVE?
SHE'S HIS COUSIN!
HE SAYS SO, AND THAT'S GOOD ENOUGH FOR YOU?
WHAT MORE DO I NEED?
VERONICA, I OWE YOU AN APOLOGY!
FOR WHAT?
I HAVE MISJUDGED YOU! I NEVER THOUGHT YOU HAD SO MUCH FAITH!
CONGRATULATIONS! AND, I EVEN HOPE IT IS HIS COUSIN!
IS THAT TRUE? ARCHIE IS RUNNING. AROUND WITH ANOTHER GIRL?
ONLY HIS COUSIN, DADDY! HE TOLD ME SHE WAS COMING!
B-BUT HOW CAN YOU BE SURE HE'S TELLING YOU THE TRUTH?
COME, DADDY!

OBSERVE! THIS IS ARCHIE'S FAMILY TREE!
ANDREWS
NOW HERE IS COUSIN SALLY! THE SECOND OF FOUR CHILDREN! BORN TO MRS. ANDREW'S YOUNGER SISTER MATILDA!
ANDREWS 1632-1960
-AND HERE IS MY FILE ON ARCHIE!
---AUNTS, UNCLES, SECOND COUSINS, FIRST COUSINS, ---
HERE IT IS!
THIS IS SALLY! HEIGHT, WEIGHT, DISCRIPTION, HISTORY! ---EVEN A PICTURE!
YOU SEE? I KNOW THAT'S THE GIRL HE WAS WITH!
EGAD! YOU'RE A TRUSTING SOUL!
WELL, OF COURSE! ISN'T THAT WHAT I'VE BEEN TELLING EVERYBODY?
THE END

Script: Frank Doyle / Pencils: Dan DeCarlo / Inks: Rudy Lapick / Letters: Vince DeCarlo

Originally printed in ARCHIE'S GIRLS BETTY & VERONICA #57, SEPTEMBER 1960

THAT WAS A SILLY QUESTION! WHAT I MEANT WAS, DID YOU SPEAK TO HIM PERSONALLY?
OF COURSE I DID! DO YOU THINK I HAVE TO GO THROUGH CHANNELS?
WHAT DID YOU SAY?
WHAT DO YOU MEAN, WHAT DID I SAY?
EXACTLY WHAT WORDS DID YOU USE?
I SAID, "HI, ARCHIEKINS! HOW ABOUT COMING OVER FOR A DIP IN MY POOL?"
UH, HUH! I THOUGHT SO!
NOW WHAT DO YOU MEAN BY THAT?

NOTHING!
EXCEPT THAT YOU DIDN'T MENTION YOUR NAME!
WHAT?
YOU NEVER SAID WHO YOU WERE!
WHO ELSE WOULD I BE?
WHO ELSE WOULD SAY, "HI, ARCHIEKINS! HOW ABOUT COMING OVER FOR A DIP IN MY POOL?"
WELL, SAY SOME-THING, GIRL!!
-WHO ELSE? WHO ELSE?---

I DON'T KNOW, RON! I WAS JUST MAKING CONVERSATION!
HMM?
AFTER ALL, ON THE PHONE I'M ONLY A FEMININE VOICE!
HE MUST KNOW OTHER GIRLS WITH FEMININE VOICES!
I DARE SAY!
---W-WHO HAVE P-POOLS!
-WHO CALL HIM, "ARCHIEKINS?"
WHY NOT? I ASK YOU, WHY NOT?
HOW DO I KNOW WHAT MAUDLIN NAMES THOSE INSIPID FEMALES USE?

WHO KNOWS HOW MANY SPOILED, RICH FEMALES HE HAS ON HIS STRING?
-BESIDES ME, I MEAN!
DO YOU KNOW WHAT I SAY, BETTY? DO YOU KNOW WHAT I SAY?
NO, RONNIE! WHAT DO YOU SAY?
I SAY, "YECH!"
LET HIM SOAK HIS BIG FAT HEAD IN EVERY POOL IN TOWN!!
HE CAN SHRIVEL LIKE A PRUNE, FOR ALL I CARE!!

HMPH! LOOK AT HIM FLOUNDERING UP HERE LIKE A FISH OUT OF WATER!
HI, GIRLS! SORRY I'M LATE!
WHAT DID YOU DO? COME OVER HERE FOR YOUR FINAL RINSE?
EEP!
SPLASH!
GLUB!! H-HEY! W-WHAT DID I DO?
AS IF YOU DIDN'T KNOW, YOU WATER-LOGGED CASANOVA!!
?
THE END

Script: Frank Doyle / Pencils: Dan DeCarlo / Inks: Rudy Lapick / Letters: Vince DeCarlo

Originally printed in ARCHIE'S GIRLS BETTY & VERONICA #59, NOVEMBER 1960

REGGIE, THIS ONE BRAZENLY ADMITS HOW SHE USES POOR ARCHIE!-- OR MISUSES HIM!
SHE SAYS WHEN HE GETS TOO SURE OF HIMSELF SHE JUST DATES SOMEONE ELSE!
WHY NOT?
THE TRICK IS TO KEEP HIM DANGLING, CONSTANTLY!
LIKE A PUPPET?
EXACTLY!
TSK, TSK! HOW AWFUL!
...CARE TO MANIPULATE MY STRINGS A BIT?
NO THANKS, REGGIE!
--YOU'D ENJOY IT TOO MUCH!
SHUCKS!

I WISH I WAS LOW-DOWN ENOUGH TO SQUEAL ON HER!
BOY! IF I WAS A TATTLE-TALE, A STOOL PIGEON! ... I'D TELL ARCHIE EXACTLY WHAT SHE SAID!
"TATTLE-TALE? STOOL PIGEON? SQUEALER?"
I NEVER HEARD A BETTER DISCRIPTION OF ME!
--WHERE IS HE?
(GASP)
REGGIE! HOW COULD YOU EVEN CONSIDER SUCH A SCURVY TRICK?
-- HE'S AT THE CHOKLIT SHOPPE!
THAT'S MY GIRL!
WELL, WELL! IF IT ISN'T THE PASSIONATE PUPPET HIMSELF!
?
3

"PUPPET"?
YOU KNOW! A BLOCKHEAD WITH STRINGS!
SOMEBODY PULLS THE STRINGS ...YOU MOVE!
WHO SAYS SO?
SODA 40¢
VERONICA!
I GOT IT STRAIGHT FROM HER RUBY LIPS!
HAH!
DO YOU EXPECT ME TO TAKE YOUR WORD?
ASK BETTY!
I'M SORRY, ARCHIE! I CANNOT TELL A LIE...!
TRY, GIRL! TRY!
4

(SIGH)--REGGIE, I WOULDN'T BELIEVE!--BUT BETTY ALWAYS LEVELS WITH ME!
TO THINK THAT MY RONNIE WOULD HAVE SUCH AN OPINION OF ME!
A PUPPET, EH?
THAT'S WHAT SHE TOLD REG AND BETTY!
HMM!--THEY PULLED A FEW STRINGS THEMSELVES!
HUH? WHAT DO YOU MEAN?
THEY MADE YOU DO JUST WHAT THEY WANTED YOU TO DO!
THEY DID?
OF COURSE! NOW THAT YOU'RE PEEVED AT RONNIE, YOU'LL PROBABLY DATE BETTY!
Y-EAH!!
5

--THAT WILL LEAVE A CLEAR FIELD FOR REGGIE TO GO AFTER VERONICA!
BY GOLLY! YOU'RE RIGHT!
WAP!
WELL, I'M SICK OF BEING PUSHED AROUND!!--I'LL SHOW THEM ALL!
YOU'VE BEEN WANTING ME TO GO FISHING, HAVEN'T YOU?
YEAH!
OKAY! WE'RE GOING!
THAT'LL TEACH THEM A LESSON!
SURE IT WILL, ARCH!
THIS IS MORE LIKE IT! FOR A CHANGE I'M DOING WHAT I WANT!
SURE YOU ARE, PAL!
WATCH IT! YOU'VE GOT A BITE!
THE END

Script: Frank Doyle / Pencils: Dan DeCarlo / Inks: Rudy Lapick / Letters: Vince DeCarlo

Originally printed in ARCHIE'S GIRLS BETTY & VERONICA #60, DECEMBER 1960

MAN! AM I GLAD WE EAVESDROPPED!
IT PAYS TO BE SNEAKY!
A FAT CHANCE THEY'VE GOT OF MAKING PACK MULES OF US!
THAT'S A POLITE TERM FOR WHAT THEY WANT TO MAKE OF US!
ER-THERE'S JUST ONE THING!
WHAT'S THAT?
WHAT IF ARCHIE AND REGGIE HEAR ABOUT IT?
HAH! WE JUST MAKE SURE THEY DON'T!
(GULP)--D-DO YOU REALIZE WHAT THAT MEANS?
T-THEY DON'T MEAN US!
--THEY'VE GOT OTHER BOYS!
R
2

SOMEBODY IS JUMPING OUR CLAIM!
HMPH! SO THE "BOYS" WILL BE THERE AT NINE, EH?
I GET THE PICTURE, PAL!
EIGHT A.M.
GOOD MORNING, SMITHERS!
IT WAS!
WHERE'S THE STUFF TO GO TO THE CABIN?
MISS VERONICA! THE FOOLS... ER-- THE "BOYS" HAVE ARRIVED!
EEP!! W-WHAT ARE YOU TWO DOING HERE?
PROTECTING OUR INTERESTS!
W-WHY, WHATEVER DO YOU MEAN?
3

HAH! AS IF YOU DIDN'T KNOW!
I SUPPOSE YOU WERE GOING TO CARRY THIS HEAVY STUFF!
--OR MAYBE YOU WERE EXPECTING SOMEONE ELSE?
WHO? US?
S-SOMEONE ELSE?
W-WERE YOU EXPECTING SOMEONE, BETTY?
NOT ME, RON!
OKAY! OKAY!
LET'S START PACKING, REG!
LET'S START HELPING, ARCH!
THEY (PUFF, PUFF) C-CAN'T S-SAY A WORD!
WE'VE GOT THEM OVER A B-BARREL!
4

GASP!
GRUNT!
GROAN!!
DID WE, (HEH, HEH) LEAVE ANYTHING BEHIND, GIRLS?
N-NO! I DON'T THINK SO!
OKAY! START UNLOADING, REG!

START HELPING, ARCH!

PUFF, PUFF!
PANT!
5

WHEW! TELL ME! HOW DID YOU GET THOSE "BOYS" TO AGREE TO THIS JOB?
WHAT BOYS?
DON'T KID US! WE KNOW!
WELL, WHOEVER THEY WERE, THEY WERE JERKS!
CAN YOU IMAGINE ANYBODY VOLUNTEERING TO DO THIS JOB?
YUK! YUK!
BOY! WHERE DO YOU MEET SUCH CHUMPS?
WHO ASKED YOU TO DO IT?
ULP! Y-YOU KNOW WHAT, REG?
I THINK I KNOW WHO THE "BOYS" ARE!
(SIGH) M-ME TOO!
6
THE END

Script: Frank Doyle / Pencils: Dan DeCarlo / Inks & Letters: Vince DeCarlo

Originally printed in ARCHIE'S GIRLS BETTY & VERONICA #61, JANUARY 1961

HOW COME? - I ASK YOU! HOW COME? A NINETY-NINE GUN SALUTE FOR YOU, AND A FINGER SNAP FOR ME!
ZEST, BETTY!
ZEST?
PUT SOME INTO YOUR GREETINGS!
ZEST, EH?
YOU NEED TO BE MORE VIVACIOUS! MORE LIVELY!
WHEN YOU SAY HELLO, SING IT OUT AS THOUGH YOU MEANT IT!
OKAY! I'LL DO IT!
ZEST, EH?
HELLO, ARCHIE! HOWSA BOY? - WHAT'S THE GOOD WORD, EH, ARCHIE BABY?
2

ER-HI, BETS!
HMPH! BIG CHANGE!
ZEST IS FOR THE BIRDS!
IT DIDN'T WORK?
LIKE A LEAD BALLOON, IT WENT OVER!
IT ALWAYS WORKS! A BOUNCY GREETING IS CONTAGIOUS! GIVE IT MORE!
OKAY! MORE IT GETS!
ARCHIE, BUDDY, PAL, CHUM! HOWSA OL' DON JUAN OF RIVERDALE? EH, BOY?
WAP!
(SIGH)-NOT BAD, BETTY!
3

NOT ENOUGH, I GUESS!
MAYBE IT NEEDS MORE TEETH!
AND--AND A SORT OF LIFT!...
HI YA!
THAT'S IT! I'LL GIVE IT ANOTHER WHIRL, AND...
OOPS!
HOT ZINGITY-ZANG! THAT'S ZEST!
4

YEAH! THOSE NEW CHEERS ARE FINE! AND THE ACROBATICS ARE GREAT!
GOOD! THE CHEERING SQUAD HAS TO LEARN THEM BY FRIDAY'S GAME!
WELL! -HERE GOES!
ARCHIE!
HIYA, BOY!
HOW'RE YOU D-DOING?
WHAT'S THE G-GOOD W-W---
CRASH!
TSK! BETTY! WHY CAN'T YOU JUST SAY A QUIET, DIGNIFIED HELLO?
...LIKE VERONICA DOES!
5
THE END

Script: Frank Doyle / Pencils: Dan DeCarlo / Inks: Rudy Lapick / Letters: Vince DeCarlo

Originally printed in ARCHIE'S GIRLS BETTY & VERONICA #64, APRIL 1961

POOR ARCHIE DOESN'T HAVE THE ADVANTAGES OF MY SOCIAL BACKGROUND!
WHO DOES?
I'M TRYING TO TEACH HIM THE RUDIMENTS OF SOCIAL BEHAVIOR!
RUDIMENTS, NO LESS!
SO THAT ONE DAY, ...IN THE FUTURE...
...IF WE SHOULD MARRY!
..HE'LL BE WORTHY OF MY STATION IN LIFE!
ALL ABOARD!!
LOOK, RONNIE! AREN'T YOU BEING A BIT...
AH! HERE HE COMES NOW!
HI, LOVER!
ARCHIE! THAT IS NO WAY TO GREET A LADY!
2

TRY IT ON ME, GOOD LOOKING!
HEY! THERE'S A LOT OF KEEN SNOW OUT THERE TODAY!
DID YOU HEAR WHAT I SAID?
LET'S GO OUT!
I'M WAITING!
WAITING? -FOR WHAT?
A GENTLEMAN OPENS A DOOR FOR A LADY!
HUH? -OH! -OH, SURE! YOU MEAN ME!
AFTER YOU, MADAM!
SPLOOSH!
3

HEY! -(SNICKER)- IT PAYS TO BE A GENTLEMAN!
TSK! REALLY, ARCHIE!
WHAT NOW?
A GENTLEMAN ALWAYS WALKS ON THE OUTSIDE!
OH!
SHUCKS! I'VE GOT NOTHING AGAINST ETIQUETTE!
-AS A MATTER OF FACT, I'M GETTING MORE SOLD ON IT EVERY MINUTE!
MY ARM, ARCHIE! MY ARM!
THAT'S WHAT IT IS, SURE ENOUGH! LOOK, BETTY! SEE RONNIE'S ARM?
OH, HOW COMMON! A GENTLEMAN IS EXPECTED TO TAKE A LADIES ARM WHILE WALKING!
OOOH! THAT!
4

WATCH IT HERE, BETTY! IT'S PRETTY SLIPPERY!
WHOOPS!
EEP!
SWISH!
WHAP!
WHEW! THANKS, RONNIE!
IF YOU HADN'T BEEN HOLDING MY ARM I MIGHT HAVE FALLEN!
GIVE UP, GIRLIE?
5

COME ON! LET'S TAKE A TABLE! RONNIE NEEDS A REST!
ARCHIE!
I EXPECT YOU TO PULL OUT MY CHAIR FOR ME!
OH! YEAH, SURE!
SAY, ARCHIE!
YEAH, POPS?
CRASH!
UH, OH!!
GULP!
ARCHIE, MY BOY! I'M AFRAID YOU JUST HAVEN'T REACHED HER STATION IN LIFE!
HOW C-CAN I, WHEN SHE KEEPS WRECKING THE TRAIN?
The End

Script: Frank Doyle / Pencils: Dan DeCarlo / Inks: Rudy Lapick / Letters: Vince DeCarlo

Originally printed in ARCHIE'S GIRLS BETTY & VERONICA #66, JUNE 1961

D-DID I CALL IT? DIDN'T I S-SAY SHE'D... ..SHE....
WHAT?
YOU SHOULD HAVE ASKED A LITTLE SOONER!
W-WELL HOW DO YOU LIKE THAT FOR INGRATITUDE! S-SHE TURNED ME DOWN!!
SO WHY GET EXCITED! THERE'S ALWAYS VERONICA!
NOT FOR TONIGHT, THERE ISN'T! I ALREADY TOLD HER I HAD SOME-THING ELSE TO DO!
SHE DIDN'T ARGUE?
SHE SAID SHE'D SORT OF HALF PROMISED TO GO BOWLING WITH ONE OF HER GIRL FRIENDS ANYWAY!
2

HMPH! THAT BETTY! TRY TO DO HER A FAVOR, AND LOOK WHAT HAPPENS!
PHOOEY!
HI, RON! I HEAR YOU'RE ROLLING A FEW FRAMES TONIGHT?
WHY, YES, JUGGIE!
I'VE BEEN PROMISING BETTY TO BOWL WITH HER FOR SO LONG, AND...
HA! HA! HA!
HOO! HEE!
HA!
HEE!
HA! HA! HA!
HEE! HOO
W-WHAT'S SO FUNNY?
B-BETTY TURNED DOWN ARCHIE, FOR A DATE WITH YOU!
WHAT?
Y-YOU MEAN SHE WAS THE SOMETHING ELSE HE HAD TO DO?
HA! HA!
HA! HA! HA! HA!
3

I'LL KILL HIM! I'LL TEAR HIM TO PIECES! I'LL TEAR THE PIECES TO... TO...
...SAY! THAT MEANS HE'S FREE NOW! AND ALL I HAVE TO GET RID OF IS BETTY!
-AND THAT COMES UNDER THE HEADING OF PLEASURE
?
YUK! YUK!
JUGGIE! W-WHY THE HILARITY?
ARCHIE DUMPED VERONICA TO DATE YOU! SEE?
-AND-AND Y-YOU TURNED HIM DOWN TO GO OUT WITH RONNIE!!
OH, NO!!!
4

THERE'S A BOO-BOO THAT'S GOING TO BE FIXED UP IN JIG TIME!
WHY, RONNIE, DARLING! HOW ARE YOU?
BETTY, ANGEL! HOW NICE TO SEE YOU!
ISN'T IT EARLY TO BE DRESSED FOR BOWLING?
YES, DARLING! I DON'T HAVE ANY OLD RAGS FOR BOWLING IN!
-I GIVE YOU ALL MY CAST OFFS!
WHY-YOU...
JUST FOR THAT, YOU CAN GO BOWLING ALONE TONIGHT!
WHY, THANK YOU!
-BUT IT ALWAYS FEELS LIKE THAT WHEN I'M WITH YOU ANYWAY!
5

HMPH!
HAH!
(GASP)-W-WHY YOU...!
OUT OF MY WAY!!
HE'S GOING OUT WITH ME!
-WITH ME!
CRASH!
(SIGH)-HE WAS GOING BOWLING WITH ME! BUT NOW,....
I'LL SPOT YOU TEN PINS EACH AND BOWL LEFTY!
FAIR ENOUGH!
ROLL, SUCKER!
The End

Script: Frank Doyle / Art: Dan DeCarlo

Originally printed in ARCHIE'S GIRLS BETTY & VERONICA #67, JULY 1961

ANGER
HUH? ...W-WHAT HAPPENED?
---YIPE!!
BETTY! -Y-YOU SAVED MY LIFE!!
W-WHY I C-COULD HAVE BEEN KILLED!
I WAS JUST LUCKY TO BE THERE!
B-BETTY! I OWE YOU MY LIFE!! H-HOW CAN I EVER REPAY YOU?
HMMMMMM!!
2

NAME IT! TELL ME SOME WAY THAT I CAN...
NOW, NOW, DON'T BE SO HASTY!
WE CAN TALK IT OVER TONIGHT, IF YOU INSIST!
T-TONIGHT?
B-BUT TONIGHT RONNIE AND I ARE...
MY! I WONDER HOW DEEP THAT AWFUL MANHOLE WAS?
...I WONDER WHAT YOU'D LOOK LIKE NOW...IF I HADN'T GRABBED YOU, AND...
(ULP!)
W-WHAT TIME SHALL I PICK YOU UP TONIGHT, BETTY?
WHY, EIGHT O'CLOCK WILL BE FINE, ARCHIE!
NOW I HOPE YOU'RE NOT GOING TO FEEL OBLIGATED TO ME, ARCHIEKINS! -- JUST BECAUSE I SAVED YOUR LIFE!!
ULP! -N-NO! NOT AT ALL!!
3

YOU'RE GOING TO **WHAT** TONIGHT?
G-GO OUT W-WITH B-BETTY!
HONEY!--SHE **SAVED** MY **LIFE!** I'M OBLIGATED TO HER!
BETTER YOU SHOULD HAVE GONE IN THE HOLE!
NOW WAIT A MINUTE...
LOOK!--SHE'S **NEVER** GOING TO LET YOU FORGET THIS!
NOT **EVER!**
I S-SUPPOSE YOU'RE RIGHT!
THERE'S ONLY ONE WAY OUT!
WHAT'S THAT?
YOU'VE GOT TO SAVE **HER** LIFE!
4

W-WHY, THAT'S GREAT! THAT WILL WIPE OUT THE OBLIGATION!
NOW, HERE'S THE WAY WE'LL DO IT!
YOU'VE SEEN THOSE MEN PAINTING MY HOUSE?
WITH THE BIG LADDER RIGHT OUTSIDE YOUR FRONT DOOR?
IN TWENTY MINUTES THEY'LL BE TAKING COFFEE BREAK!
THAT'S WHEN YOU BRING BETTY OVER!
NOW SUPPOSE A HEAVY PAINT CAN DROPPED FROM THE TOP OF THE LADDER!
-AND CAME HURTLING DOWN! ...RIGHT AT BETTY!!
I GET IT! I GET IT!
--AND I SAVE HER IN THE NICK OF TIME!
EXACTLY!
5

I'LL LEAN OUT THE UPSTAIRS WINDOW!--SEE?
SO YOU CAN REACH THE PAINT CAN!
WHEN I SEE YOU DRAG HER OUT OF THE WAY,...I'LL DROP THE CAN, AND...
WATCH IT!!
WHOOSH!
WHAM!
T-THE PAINTER DROPPED IT JUST AS YOU STEPPED OUT THE DOOR! IT'S LUCKY I WAS PASSING!
(GULP)--RONNIE! N-NOW SHE'S SAVED Y-YOUR LIFE, TOO
I KNOW, ARCHIE! I KNOW!
(SIGH)--I GUESS THIS JUST ISN'T ONE OF OUR LUCKY DAYS!
?
The End

Script: Frank Doyle / Pencils: Dan DeCarlo / Inks & Letters: Vince DeCarlo

Originally printed in ARCHIE'S GIRLS BETTY & VERONICA #69, SEPTEMBER 1961

I'LL TELL YOU WHO I HATE LIKE THAT!
ARCHIE!
NO-O-OOOO!!
I KNEW YOU'D BE SURPRISED!
DO YOU KNOW WHY?
I COULDN'T GUESS!
HE SAID I HAD A LOT IN COMMON WITH VENUS DE MILO!
THAT SOUNDS LIKE A RATHER EXTRAVAGANT COMPLIMENT TO ME!
"COMPLIMENT"?
...USING THE WORD COMMON WHEN REFERRING TO ME?
2

IF YOU SEE HIM, TELL HIM I NEVER WANT TO SEE HIM AGAIN!
ARE YOU SURE THAT...
I'M SURE!
ARCHIE! I'M THE BEARER OF GOOD TIDINGS!
VERONICA SAYS SHE NEVER WANTS TO SEE YOU AGAIN!
WHY?
BECAUSE YOU REFERRED TO HER AS "COMMON"!
THAT'S NONSENSE, BETTY!
SHE COULDN'T HAVE CONSIDERED WHAT I SAID AN INSULT! NOBODY COULD BE THAT DUMB!
THAT'S WHAT HE SAID, RONNIE! WORD FOR WORD!
DUMB, EH?
3

WELL I'M SMART ENOUGH TO DROP HIM LIKE A BAD HABIT!
RONNIE! NO!
HE DIDN'T MEAN IT LIKE THAT!
IF YOU'RE MY FRIEND, YOU'LL TELL HIM WHAT I SAID!
DID SHE STOP POUTING YET?
NOT EXACTLY!
SHE SAID SHE'S DROPPING YOU LIKE A BAD HABIT!
ULP! S-SHE SAID THAT?
LOOK, BETTY! TELL HER I TAKE BACK WHAT I SAID!
OKAY!
4

YOU THINK I'M OUT OF MY MIND TO TRY TO PATCH UP THIS QUARREL?
THE WAY RONNIE TWISTS THINGS AROUND, ARCHIE WILL LAND RIGHT IN MY LAP!
ARCHIE SAYS HE TAKES BACK WHAT HE SAID!
PUFF PUFF
WHAT?
HE SAID NOBODY COULD BE THAT DUMB!
...THAT MEANS HE THINKS SOMEBODY COULD BE THAT DUMB!
-NAMELY ME!
NOW, RON...
5

I'LL SEE HIM PERSONALLY ABOUT THIS!
SEE? NOW I JUST SIT AND WAIT!
I'LL CATCH HIM ON THE FIRST BOUNCE!
B-BUT RONNIE! I APOLOGIZED!
YOU DID?
DIDN'T BETTY TELL YOU?
SHE BROUGHT ME NOTHING BUT INSULTS!
EEP!!
HMPH! TROUBLEMAKER!
?
The End

Script: Frank Doyle / Pencils: Dan DeCarlo / Inks & Letters: Vince DeCarlo

Originally printed in ARCHIE'S GIRLS BETTY & VERONICA #70, OCTOBER 1961

PISH POSH! WHAT KIND OF MONSTER COULD POSSIBLY FRIGHTEN US?
-WE GREW UP WITH YOU AND REGGIE AND JUGHEAD!
HMPH! MY SYMPATHY IS WITH THE MONSTER!
MONSTERS, INDEED! WHAT KIND OF FOOLS DOES HE TAKE US FOR?
FUNNY HOW YOUR IMAGINATION PLAYS TRICKS ON YOU, THOUGH!
LOOK! DOESN'T THAT HILL ON THE ISLAND LOOK LIKE SOME SORT OF BIG BEAST?
(GIGGLE) IT DOES AT THAT!
2

LET'S FIND A GOOD PLACE TO EAT OUR LUNCH!
I'M GOING TO SIT ON THIS ROCK! TOO MANY CRAWLING THINGS ON THE GROUND!
I'M WITH **YOU**, GIRL!
THIS SURE IS A SMOOTH ROCK!
HA! IT LOOKS LIKE A BIG EGG!
OF COURSE! A MONSTER EGG!
MAYBE WE'LL **HATCH** IT!
HEE, HEE! S-STOP IT, B-BETTY!
I'M GOING TO SAVE SOME FOR LATER!
GOOD IDEA! LET'S EXPLORE THE ISLAND!
C-R-RACK!
3

D-DO YOU HAVE A FUNNY FEELING?
L-LIKE WE'RE BEING **F-FOLLOWED?**
Y-YES! T-TAKE A QUICK LOOK!
N-NOT ME! **YOU** LOOK!
W-WE'LL **BOTH** LOOK!
WHEW! N-NOTHING!
NOTHING BUT IMAGINATION!
4

WOULDN'T ARCHIE LAUGH IF HE KNEW HOW JUMPY HE'D MADE US!
I'LL BET THAT WAS HIS WHOLE PURPOSE IN MENTIONING MONSTERS!
CHUMP! CHUMP!
B-BETTY! D-DID YOU EAT THE REST OF OUR LUNCH?
N-NO! DIDN'T YOU?
L-LET'S G-GET OUT OF HERE!
5

WHAT EVER YOU DO, DON'T TELL ARCHIE WE WERE FRIGHTENED OFF THE ISLAND!
DO YOU THINK I'M CRAZY?
Y-YOU DON'T S-SUPPOSE THERE WAS SOME SORT OF...
BETTY! DON'T BE RIDICULOUS!
THERE ARE NO SUCH THINGS AS MONSTERS!
* OMMAM! EY ASW WOT STERONS NON ATH EABE!
*TRANSLATION: M-MOMMA! I S-SAW TWO MONSTERS ON THE B-BEACH!
CENSNON NSO! ER THO ERA ONO SUH INO STH SAG STERMON!
*...NONSENSE, SON! THERE ARE NO SUCH THINGS AS MONSTERS!
The End

Script: Frank Doyle / Pencils: Dan DeCarlo / Inks: Rudy Lapick / Letters: Vince DeCarlo

Originally printed in ARCHIE'S GIRLS BETTY & VERONICA #73, JANUARY 1962

IT'S THOSE MOVIE WRITERS WITH THEIR WILD IMAGINATIONS!
THEY MAKE PEOPLE BELIEVE IN ALL SORTS OF NONSENSE!
IF WE HAD SEEN THAT PICTURE WE'D PROBABLY THINK THAT WAS THE SHADOW OF A MONSTER!
YES!
WHILE IT'S PROBABLY A BUSH OR A TREE!
OF COURSE!
EVEN TODAY, SOME FOLKS ARE VERY BACKWARD!
HOW TRUE! THEY SIMPLY WON'T LET GO OF THEIR ANCIENT, SUPERSTITIOUS BELIEFS!
COME ON IN AND HAVE SOME HOT CHOCOLATE!
I'D LOVE TO!
2

ALL ONE NEEDS IN ORDER TO BE SCARED, IS A VIVID IMAGINATION!
-AND A CERTAIN DEGREE OF STUPIDITY!
GRUNT! SNORT
PANT! GEEP!
WHEEZ
GRR
BING! BONG!
YES! I SUPPOSE SUCH PEOPLE ARE STUPID!
GRUNT!
WELL? WHAT IS IT YOU WANT, MISTER? I CAN'T STAND HERE ALL NIGHT WITH THE DOOR OPEN!
HE OBVIOUSLY WANTS A HANDOUT! THE POOR MAN! LOOK AT THAT MOTH EATEN OLD FUR COAT HE'S WEARING!

OF COURSE! THAT'S IT!
STEP IN OUT OF THE COLD, SIR! HAVE SOME HOT CHOCOLATE AN COOKIES!
LET ME TAKE YOUR COAT!
ER-N-NO! I T-THINK I'LL KEEP IT ON!
WE WERE TALKING ABOUT MONSTERS!
YOU DON'T BELIEVE IN MONSTERS, DO YOU?
ER-AH... Y-YES! I DO!
YOU POOR MAN! DON'T YOU KNOW MONSTERS ARE IMAGINARY?
GLUP! W-WE ARE?
ER-I-M-MEAN... REALLY?
4

SUPPOSE YOU SAW A BIG HAIRY CREATURE COMING AT YOU LIKE THIS?
...SNARL!! SNORT!! GRRRROOWL!!
(GIGGLE) HE'S GOOD!
W-WOULDN'T THIS SCARE YOU?
EEEE! YOUR FUR COAT TICKLES!
HEE, HEE! THAT'S WONDERFUL, MISTER! BUT YOU DON'T HAVE TO PERFORM TO PAY FOR YOUR SNACK!
(SIGH!)
NOW YOU CALL, ANYTIME YOU'RE IN THE NEIGHBORHOOD, ...YOU HEAR?
IT'S POOR UNDERPRIVILEGED TYPES LIKE THAT WHO BELIEVE IN MONSTERS!
YOU'RE SO RIGHT!
SOB!
The End

Script: Frank Doyle / Pencils: Dan DeCarlo / Inks: Rudy Lapick / Letters: Vince DeCarlo

Originally printed in ARCHIE'S GIRLS BETTY & VERONICA #74, FEBRUARY 1962

WAIT TILL I TELL VERONICA!
RONNIE! GUESS WHAT I....
LOOK, BETTY!
DO YOU KNOW WHAT THAT IS?
ULP!
THAT'S THE EXACT SHADE OF GREEN OF MY NEW SKIRT!
ISN'T IT LOVELY?
Y-YEAH! JUST LOVELY!
2

WAIT UNTIL YOU SEE IT! I'M WEARING IT SATURDAY NIGHT!
ER-EXCUSE ME, RON!
I'VE SIMPLY GOT TO RUN!
?
AHA! I THOUGHT SO!
YOU WANT TO GET THE SAME COLOR AS I HAVE!
(SIGH)-RONNIE! WHAT I WANTED WAS THE FIVE DOLLARS!
5
WHATEVER FOR?
3

WHY DOES ANYONE WANT FIVE DOLLARS?
I WASN'T AWARE THAT THEY DID!
IT'S MONEY, GIRL!
PEOPLE NEED MONEY!
HAVEN'T THEY GOT SOME?
GIVE ME STRENGTH!
NOT ENOUGH TO PASS UP FIVE DOLLARS!
TSK, TSK!
POOR BETTY! YOU HAVE SUCH A LOW OPINION OF PEOPLE!
NOBODY NEEDS FIVE DOLLARS BADLY ENOUGH TO PICK IT OFF THE STREET!
OH, NO?
4

YOU JUST WATCH!
DOES THIS BELONG TO ONE OF YOU GIRLS?
NO!
SURELY YOU'RE NOT GOING TO KEEP THAT FILTHY BILL?
ARE YOU NUTS?
SEE?
IT'S A CITIZENS DUTY TO KEEP THE STREETS CLEAN!
I CAN'T STAND A LITTERBUG!
5

NOW CUT THAT OUT! WHO DO YOU THINK YOU'RE KIDDING?
WHY NOBODY!
THEN WHAT ARE YOU GOING TO DO WITH THAT?
THIS DIRTY SCRAP OF PAPER WHICH SOMEBODY CARE-LESSLY DROPPED ON THE STREET?
R
R
WHY I'M GOING TO GET RID OF IT!
SEE?
COME ON, RONNIE!
R
I BELIEVE I CAN DISPOSE OF IT FASTER WITH YOUR HELP!
AS YOU CAN SEE, I'M NO LITTERBUG!
KEEP YOUR CITY CLEAN
The End

Script: Frank Doyle / Pencils: Dan DeCarlo / Inks: Rudy Lapick / Letters: Vince DeCarlo

Originally printed in ARCHIE'S GIRLS BETTY & VERONICA #74, FEBRUARY 1962

HAH! IF WISHES WERE HORSES, BEGGARS WOULD RIDE!
DARN, WHY DON'T THEY HAVE FAIRY GODMOTHERS OR SOMETHING?
-HOW ABOUT A FAIRY GODFATHER?
HUH?
POP!
W-WHO ARE YOU?
I'M ONE OF THOSE CHARACTERS THAT NO ONE EVER TAKES SERIOUSLY!
Y-YOU S-SAID FAIRY GODFATHER!!
-AND YOU THINK I'M SOME SORT OF A NUT!
YOU SAID IT, MISTER! I DIDN'T!
ALL RIGHT! LAUGH THIS OFF!
(YAWN)
H-HE'S GONE!
POP!
2

SAY! YOU'RE A COOL ONE!
D-D-D-UH..!!
NOW DON'T SCURRY, LITTLE BUNNY! IT'S ONLY YOUR OWN CHRIS!
B-B-BUT...
SURE! YOU MADE ME WHAT I AM TODAY, PIGEON!
HI, RON! DO I KNOW YOUR FRIEND?
ER-OH, ARCHIE!
T-THIS IS CHRIS!
EEYIKES! WHAT A COLD GRIP!!
THE BETTER TO FREEZE YOU OUT, CHUMP!
C'MON DOLL, LET'S SHAKE HOT BLOODED HARRY HERE!
WHATEVER Y-YOU SAY, CHRIS!
3

SWALLOW A HORNETS NEST, ARCHIE?
T-THAT VERONICA! S-SHE'S GOT A NEW ONE!
WHO?
SOME BIG HANDSOME JERK NAMED CHRIS!
"CHRIS?" THIS I'VE GOT TO SEE!
IT COULDN'T BE! IT JUST COULDN'T...
...(GASP) B-BUT IT IS!!
HELLO DAHLING!
R-RON! IT'S CRAZY! IMPOSSIBLE! I'M DREAMING!
NEVER UNDERESTIMATE THE POWER OF A WOMAN, LITTLE GIRL!
4

(SIGH)-I CAN'T BELIEVE IT MYSELF!
I REALLY DID A BEAUTIFUL JOB ON YOU!
ALLOW ME TO RETURN THE FAVOR, CHICK!
SMACK!
I'LL BE BACK WHEN YOU'VE THAWED OUT, BABY!
GOOD GRIEF!-RONNIE! W-WHAT HAPPENED?
C-CHRIS K-K-KISSED M-ME!
5

B-BETTY! WHAT WILL I D-DO?
UNDERNEATH THAT GORGEOUS EXTERIOR HE'S STILL A SNOWMAN!
WELL, AFTER THE WAY YOU TREATED ME I SHOULDN'T, BUT... WHICH WAY DID HE GO?
T-THAT W-WAY!
ALL RIGHT, ADONIS! LET'S SEE WHAT SORT OF STUFF YOU'RE MADE OF!
YOU ASKED FOR IT, BLONDIE!
SMEERP!
EEK! B-BETTY! HE'S MELTING!!
NATCH!
-NEVER UNDERESTIMATE THE POWER OF A WOMAN, LITTLE ONE!
SSSSSSS
The End

Script: Frank Doyle / Pencils: Dan DeCarlo / Inks: Rudy Lapick / Letters: Vince DeCarlo

Originally printed in ARCHIE'S GIRLS BETTY & VERONICA #77, MAY 1962

THERE WILL BE NO OTHER WOMEN IN YOUR LIFE! YOU WILL ONLY HAVE EYES FOR ME!
ONLY... ...FOR... ..YOU...
NICE, HYSTERICAL, LAST DITCH EFFORT, BETTY!
CARE TO WAGER ON THE RESULTS?
EVERY DOG HAS HIS DAY, AND YOU'VE HAD YOURS!
-SO RUN ALONG AND BURY A BONE SOMEWHERE!
SNAP!
VERONICA!!
W-WHERE DID YOU LEARN HYPNOSIS?
HUH?
THIS SILLY GIRL HYPNOTIZES ME AND TELLS ME I LOVE HER!
2

YOU FRECKLE-FACED, RABBIT-TOOTHED NINNY! I WAS THE ONE WHO HYPNOTIZED YOU!!!
ULP!
W-WELL HOW WAS I TO KNOW?
I WAS IN A TRANCE!
SOMETHING HAS GONE AWRY! I CAN TELL BY YOUR PETULANT PUSS!
HYPNOSIS! BAH!
...AND WHEN HE WAKES, HE FEELS SO MUCH IN LOVE HE FIGURES IT MUST HAVE BEEN RONNIE WHO DID IT!
TSK!
YOU WERE ON THE WRONG TRACK FROM THE START!
-SO THROW THE RIGHT SWITCH!
HYPNOTIZE VERONICA!
3

OF COURSE! THERE'S MORE THAN ONE WAY TO SKIN A CAT!
-AND I KNOW ONE KITTY WHO'S ABOUT TO BE PARTED FROM HER PELT!
...DROWSY...SLEEPY... ...WEARY....
YOU DO NOT LOVE HIM!
YOU WILL FORGET YOU EVER MET HIM!
YOU CAN'T STAND THE SIGHT OF HIM!
UGH! HE'S AWFUL!
SNAP!
OMIGOSH! THE PHONE! QUICKLY!
4

ARCHIE! IT'S ALL OFF! I DON'T LOVE **HIM** ANYMORE!
HONESTLY! GOOD OL' BETTY **CURED** ME! HE'S OUT OF MY LIFE FOREVER!
W-WHO?
I FELL IN LOVE WITH ANOTHER BOY!
I HAD JUST BROKEN OFF WITH ARCHIE!
-BUT, THANKS TO **YOU,** ARCHIE AND I ARE A SET AGAIN!
...I AM A HANDSOME, RED SALMON!
I AM GOING UPSTREAM TO SPAWN!
HEH! HEH!
S
S
The End

Script: Frank Doyle / Pencils: Dan DeCarlo / Inks: Rudy Lapick / Letters: Vince DeCarlo

Originally printed in ARCHIE'S GIRLS BETTY & VERONICA #82, OCTOBER 1962

Y-YOU'RE KIDDING!!
SO HELP ME! THAT'S WHAT SHE CALLS HIM!
P-POOPSIE! YOK, YOK!
OH, WAIT TILL THE BOYS HEAR THIS!
POOPSIE?
S-SECRET PET NAME?
OOH, OOH!
QUIET! I THINK I'M GETTING A FLASH!
HEY! MIGHTY MITE! YOU WANT TO EARN TWO-BITS?
SHOW ME THE COLOR OF THE COIN, BIG MAN!
DELIVER THIS NOTE TO RONNIE LODGE, BUT DON'T TELL HER I SENT IT!
NOT MENTIONING YOU IS MY FAVORITE PAS-TIME, SLICK TOP!
2

"MEET ME AT GRANITE COVE FOR A DIP! WE'LL BE ALONE TOGETHER!" SIGNED, "POOPSIE!"
WHOOPSIE?
NEVER MIND, LITTLE MAN! IT'S A RENDEZVOUS WITH ROMANCE!
YOU KNOW, THAT WAS A GOOD GAG OF REGGIE'S, BUT IT DOESN'T HAVE TO STOP THERE!
HUH?
HERE'S YOUR QUARTER! SAME PLACE, SAME GIRL, SAME TIGHT LIP!
SILENCE IS INDEED GOLDEN!
"CHANGE OF PLANS! MEET ME AT THE BOAT DOCK FOR A SPIN! POOPSIE!"
OH, WELL, I'D BETTER SLIP INTO SOMETHING NAUTICAL!
3

HMM? NO REASON WHY I SHOULD BE LEFT OUT OF THIS!
YOU KNOW THE WAY BY NOW?
MONEY IMPROVES MY SENSE OF DIRECTION!
YOU SNICKER WITH GLEE, CHARLIE! WHAT'S UP?
YOK YOK
W-WAIT'LL I TELL YOU!
YUK! YUK!
HA! HA! HOO! HOO!
"POOPSIE?"
YOU'RE LOOKING AT THE LATEST OF A LONG LINE!
TSK! THAT LUSCIOUS RONNIE AND THAT CREEPY CHARLIE!
SHE DESERVES BETTER THAN THAT!
-NOW WHERE IS THAT KID?
4

OH, NO! DID HE CHANGE HIS MIND AGAIN?
POOPSIE IS PRETTY CHANGEABLE!
(SIGH)-ALL RIGHT! SO IT'S HORSEBACK RIDING! I HOPE THIS IS THE LAST....
...OH, NO!
OH, YES!
ANOTHER NOTE?
TENNIS THIS TIME!
THIS IS IT! THE LAST TIME!
-AND THEY SAY **WOMEN** CHANGE THEIR MINDS!
5

TENNIS, RONNIE? IN THIS HEAT?
OH, NO?!
LOOK! WHY DON'T YOU SLIP INTO A SUIT! WE SNEAK OFF TO GRANITE COVE, JUST THE TWO OF US, AND....
A SIMPLE "NO" WOULD HAVE BEEN SUFFICIENT!
POPS! A SODA FOR MY SAD FRIEND, POOPSIE!
HOW DID YOU KNOW I WAS CALLED POOPSIE!
ISN'T EVERYONE?
The End

Script: Frank Doyle / Pencils: Dan DeCarlo / Inks: Rudy Lapick / Letters: Vince DeCarlo

Originally printed in ARCHIE'S GIRLS BETTY & VERONICA #85, JANUARY 1963

TSK! YOU STOP AT MY HOUSE AT THREE O'CLOCK!
OUR FAMILY DOCTOR IS GIVING DADDY A CHECK-UP TODAY!
I'LL HAVE HIM LOOK YOU OVER!
B-BUT THERE'S NOTHING WRONG WITH ME!!
THREE O'CLOCK! YOU BE THERE!
OKAY, ANNIE OAKLEY! WHO'S THE TARGET?
LOOK, BUT DON'T TOUCH!
HIS NAME IS MICKEY MORSE!
HE REPRESENTS NEW TERRITORY THAT NEEDS EXPLORING!
R
2

NATURALLY, I DON'T WANT TO HURT ARCHIE'S FEELINGS, ...
-AND, YOU DON'T WANT TO GET **CAUGHT!**
WHAT ARCHIE DOESN'T KNOW, WON'T HURT HIM! IGNORANCE IS BLISS!
YOU SHOULD KNOW, HAPPY GIRL!
LATER:
DOCTOR, I'D LIKE YOU TO MAKE A FEW MEDICAL PASSES OVER ARCHIE!
HE'S NOT WELL?
HE NEEDS A FEW DAYS REST! OUT IN THE COUNTRY!
BUT, IF HE'S NOT **ILL...!**
OH, HE'S ILL, ALL RIGHT! HE'S GOT THIS NERVOUS HABIT!
HE KEEPS CRAMPING MY STYLE!
TSK! YOU'RE AS RUTHLESS AS YOUR FATHER!
3

B-BUT, DOC! I FEEL FINE!
SSH!
YOU'D BETTER GET AWAY FOR A FEW DAYS, SON! ER-FOR YOUR HEALTH!
HECK! WHERE COULD I **GO?**
DADDY'S CABIN! YOU CAN FISH AND RELAX!
TAKE A FRIEND WITH YOU!
?
YOU'LL COME BACK MONDAY FEELING LIKE A NEW MAN!
(SIGH)-OKAY! IF YOU INSIST!
BUT I STILL DON'T THINK I'M SICK!
I GUESS I COULD CALL IT PREVENTATIVE MEDICINE! HE **WOULD** BE SICK IF HE STAYED TO FIND OUT WHAT-EVER IT IS **YOU'RE** UP TO!
4

NEXT DAY:
THE BEST LAID PLANS OF MICE AND MEN OFTEN BLOW UP IN YOUR FACE!
WHAT DO YOU MEAN? MY PLANS WORKED OUT PERFECTLY!
ARCHIE'S UP THERE, PROBABLY WITH JUGGIE, AND....
CORRECTION, PLEASE!
JUGGIE!!
ARCHIE DIDN'T TAKE YOU? HIS BEST FRIEND?
HE WANTED TO!
BUT HE SAID HE THOUGHT IT BETTER IF HE TOOK THAT GUY, MICKEY MORSE!
5
-SO YOU COULD HAVE A QUIET WEEKEND, TOO!
THE END

Script: Frank Doyle / Pencils: Dan DeCarlo / Inks: Rudy Lapick / Letters: Vince DeCarlo

Originally printed in ARCHIE'S GIRLS BETTY & VERONICA #90, JUNE 1963

W-ELL, MAYBE SO! ANYWAY, HERE'S A PICTURE OF BETTY, COVERED BY **ME**!
AS YOU CAN SEE, I'M THE COMMON, EVERYDAY TYPE!
R
WHEN I GET ARCHIE, IT'S IN BROAD DAYLIGHT!
R
WE DO ORDINARY THINGS, LIKE SIPPING SODAS!
NOTHING REALLY EXCITING! I'M NOT THE EXCITING **TYPE**!
SODA
R
AT LEAST, NOT LIKE WHAT'S HER-NAME ON THE NEXT PAGE!
2

WHEN VERONICA SLITHERS INTO ME, THINGS HAPPEN!
BING!
BONG!
WAP!
CRASH!
POW!
THUD!
YOU DON'T GET ACTION LIKE THAT WITH A BARGAIN BASEMENT COPY!
3

OF COURSE, I'M FOR DAYTIME USE! ALL OPEN AND ABOVE BOARD!
I'M VERY MUCH AT HOME WITH ARCHIE'S OLD SWEATER AND CHECKERED TROUSERS!
R
WE HAVE FUN TOGETHER! GOOD CLEAN OUTDOOR FUN!
R
THAT ONE IS LIKE A DRACULA WHO PREYS ON INNOCENT VICTIMS!
SHE DOES HER WORK AFTER DARK!
REALLY, MY DEAR, DO YOU CONSIDER WHAT I DO, "WORK?"
4

HER ONLY CONTACT IS WITH ARCHIE'S STIFF AND UNFAMILIAR SUITS!
EVERYTHING FORMAL AND CORRECT, AS IT SHOULD BE!
AH! BUT THAT'S NOT ARCHIE!
YOU DON'T EVER GET TO KNOW THE REAL ARCHIE!
OH, BE QUIET, PEASANT!
-OR I'LL UNRAVEL YOU!
THERE'S ONE THING ABOUT BEING ONE OF THE COMMON HERD!
-YOU CAN REALLY LET YOURSELF GO!
WHOOPS!
5
The END

Script: Frank Doyle / Pencils: Dan DeCarlo / Inks: Rudy Lapick / Letters: Vince DeCarlo

Originally printed in ARCHIE'S GIRLS BETTY & VERONICA #92, AUGUST 1963

SPLUT!! SPLUTTER PTOOIE!!
LOOK AT THAT HAPPY, SMILING FACE! LISTEN TO THAT LIGHT-HEARTED LAUGHTER!!
WHY DON'T YOU TWO INFANTS GO PLAY IN DEEP WATER!
GO FIND SOMEONE ELSE TO TORMENT!
I'M TIRED!
AWIGHT, WIDDLE WONNIE! LET'S GO AN PWAY INNA SAND! FROW ME THAT PAIL!
AWIGHT, BETTY!
OOPS! THERE WAS WATER IN IT!
TISH, TUSH!
2

MAD, CRAZY FEMALES!! WHY CAN'T YOU TAKE A HINT ?

I GIVE UP! THE BEACH IS YOURS! **ALL** OF IT!

MAYBE I'LL FIND PEACE IN THE BRINY DEEP!

AH! ALONE AT LAST!

SPLOOSH!

S

FUNNY! OH, SO VERY, VERY FUNNY!!
WHEN THOSE TWO GET KITTENISH THERE'S JUST NO STOPPING THEM!
?
UH, OH!
HAH! GOT THE DROP ON YOU THAT TIME!
4

HOW DO YOU LIKE GETTING A DOSE OF YOUR OWN MEDICINE FOR A CHANGE?
WHY? IS SHE ILL?
HUH?
OMIGOSH! WHO ARE YOU!
MY! YOU ARE IMPULSIVE, AREN'T YOU!?
GOLLY! I'M SORRY! I APOLOGIZE! WHAT CAN I DO TO SHOW YOU HOW SORRY I AM?
WELL, LET'S STROLL ALONG THE BEACH! MAYBE I'LL THINK OF SOMETHING!
(SIGH) YOU KNOW, RONNIE, MAYBE WE SHOULD HAVE LET SLEEPING DOGS LIE!
HMPH!
5
IF I KNOW THAT PARTICULAR DOG, THAT'S WHAT HE'S DOING RIGHT NOW!
LYING!
END

Script: Frank Doyle / Pencils: Dan DeCarlo / Inks & Letters: Vince DeCarlo

Originally printed in ARCHIE'S GIRLS BETTY & VERONICA #92, AUGUST 1963

BING BONG
RONNIE! LOOK!!
I GATHER YOU ARE NOT AT HOME, MISS VERONICA!
YOU GATHER RIGHT, SMITHERS!
IT'S ALWAYS A PLEASURE NOT TO LET THOSE TWO IN!
IT'S NOT "THOSE TWO," IT'S REGGIE!
REGGIE WALKED RIGHT ON BY!
EEP! QUICK! OPEN THE DOOR!!
2

WELL, NO TIME FOR IDLE CHIT-CHAT, WE'RE LATE ALREADY!
FOR WHAT?
JUG AND I ARE SUPPOSED TO PUT UP NEW NETS AT THE SCHOOL TENNIS COURTS!
YOU TWO PROMISED TO HELP US SET THEM AT THE RIGHT HEIGHT!
THEY'RE RIGHT! I HAD FORGOTTEN!
WELL, LET'S GO! A PROMISE IS A PROMISE!
HEY! GREAT WHITE DADDIO! HOLD THIS A SECOND!
IT LOOKS LIKE A TENNIS NET!
IT IS! THERE'S A BUNCH OF OLD ONES IN THE TRASH CAN AT SCHOOL!
YOU GRAB IT TOO, BUGLE BEAK!
3

WHAT ARE YOU GOING TO DO WITH A BROKEN DOWN, NO GOOD TENNIS NET?
THAT'S A GOOD QUESTION!
I CAN'T THINK OF ANY GOOD ANSWER!
HEY!!
SO I THINK I'LL JUST LEAVE IT RIGHT HERE!
LADIES! YOU LOOK AS THOUGH YOU COULD USE AN ESCORT!
I ALWAYS KNEW THAT SOMEDAY A MAN WITH A NET WOULD COME AFTER THEM!
BUT I NEVER DREAMED I WOULD HAVE THE PLEASURE!
WELL? WHERE TO?
4

I FEEL FOOLISH! DO YOU?
I'VE DONE SMARTER THINGS IN MY DAY!
HOWEVER, I LIKE TO LOOK AT THE BRIGHT SIDE!
YEAH! THE REVENGE!
--TO WORK? YOU'RE PUTTING ME ON!!
THAT'S WHAT ARCHIE AND JUGGIE WERE GOING TO DO!
SHUCKS! MY TIMING SURE WAS OFF THIS TIME!
WHEW! THIS IS NO PICNIC! HURRY UP WILL YOU?
HOLD IT THERE, REGGIE!
STOP COMPLAINING! THERE'S ONLY ONE MORE TO GO!
GOOD!
5

ALLOW US, OLD BOY!
YOU'VE BEEN TOO KIND ALREADY!
GOOD! YOU'RE NOT SORE? AFTER ALL, I TIED YOU UP, BUT I ALSO DID YOUR WORK! I FIGURE WE'RE PRETTY EVEN!
WHO'S ARGUING?!
A LITTLE TIGHTER, ARCH?
GRUNT! UGH!
I GUESS THAT ABOUT WINDS IT UP!
DON'T YOU THINK IT'S A BIT TWISTED?
IS IT? I HADN'T NOTICED!
ONE GOOD TWIST DESERVES ANOTHER!
HALP!!
The End
6

Script: Frank Doyle / Pencils: Dan DeCarlo / Inks: Rudy Lapick / Letters: Vince DeCarlo

Originally printed in ARCHIE'S GIRLS BETTY & VERONICA #96, DECEMBER 1963

YOU ACT LIKE A COUPLE OF HOOLIGANS, FIGHTING OVER A SIMPERING NUT!
ANYMORE OF IT AND YOU KNOW WHAT WILL HAPPEN ON THE FRENCH CLUB MOTOR TRIP NEXT WEEK!
WHAT WILL HAPPEN ON THE FRENCH CLUB MOTOR TRIP NEXT WEEK?
PRINCIPAL
OODLES OF THINGS!
INTERESTING, FASCINATING, EXCITING THINGS!
BUT WE WON'T EXPERIENCE THEM!
WHY NOT?
BECAUSE WE WON'T BE ALLOWED TO GO IF WE FIGHT OVER ARCHIE!
OH! SO THAT'S WHAT HE MEANT!
2

GOLLY! I DON'T WANT TO MISS THAT TRIP! YOU TAKE ARCHIE THIS WEEK!
I DON'T WANT TO MISS IT EITHER!
YOU TAKE ARCHIE!
NOW LISTEN YOU! YOU'RE ALWAYS WANTING HIM! HOW COME...
...AND I'LL WANT HIM AGAIN, TOO!
..BUT AFTER THE TRIP! I'M NOT TAKING ANY CHANCES ON...
HOLD IT! STOP! CEASE! DESIST!
WE'RE DOING IT AGAIN! JUST WHAT MR. WEATHERBEE WARNED US ABOUT!
YOU'RE RIGHT! WE'RE FIGHTING OVER ARCHIE AGAIN!
BUT THIS TIME IT'S IN REVERSE!
WE'RE BOTH TRYING TO GET RID OF HIM!
3

DUCK! HERE HE COMES!
BROOM CLOSET
THE SAFEST THING TO DO IS TO AVOID HIM COMPLETELY UNTIL THE MOTOR TRIP IS OVER!
IT'S THE ONLY WAY TO KEEP FROM FIGHTING!
SEEN THE GIRLS, JUG?
PLEASE, ARCH! I JUST ATE!
BOY! WHAT A WOMAN HATER!
HAVE YOU SEEN BETTY OR VERONICA, REGGIE?
?
WOULD I TELL YOU, FRECKLE SNOOT?
4

I'VE DONE IT MISS GRUNDY! EVEN IF IT'S ONLY TEMPORARY!
DONE **WHAT**, SHE QUERIED?
I'VE GOTTEN BETTY AND VERONICA TO ACT LIKE LADIES OVER THAT ARCHIE!
REALLY? THEY LOOK MORE LIKE A COUPLE OF SNEAK THIEVES FROM HERE!
EEP!!
W-ELL, LADIES WALK ON TIPTOE SOMETI...
WHAM
5

GREAT WORK, PROFESSOR! THEY WERE RUNNING AWAY FROM ARCHIE!
IF YOU ASK ME, THEY ACTED BETTER WHEN THEY WERE FIGHTING OVER HIM!
GIRLS, YOU'RE DOING A GREAT JOB OF NOT FIGHTING OVER ARCHIE! HOWEVER, I HAVE ONE FINAL WORD ON THE SUBJECT!
YES, MR. WEATHERBEE?
6
FIGHT!
!?
END

Script: Frank Doyle / Pencils: Dan DeCarlo / Inks: Rudy Lapick / Letters: Vince DeCarlo

Originally printed in ARCHIE'S GIRLS BETTY & VERONICA #98, FEBRUARY 1964

BOING!
D-UH!..ER..
UH...AH...
I THINK HE'S TRYING TO SAY SOMETHING!
I'LL GET MY SKATES!
LIKE THE MAN SAID,... WHERE DO YOU GET THESE STUPID IDEAS?
ALL SET, LOVER DOLL!! MAN, IT'S A BEEEAUTIFUL DAY FOR SKATING!
IF I WASN'T SO MAD ABOUT HIM, I'D KILL HIM!
2

GREETINGS, FELLOW IDIOTS! WELCOME TO PNEUMONIA GULCH!
HOW'S THE SKATING?
DON'T LOOK AT ME, SPORTS LOVER! YOU'RE TALKING TO THE KEEPER OF THE FLAME!
WOW!! THAT'S BEAUTIFUL, RONNIE! MAN! LOOK AT THAT FORM!
HMPH! STEP ASIDE, REGGIE!
!?
ARE YOU WATCHING, ARCHIE DARLING?
3

I'LL SHOW YOU SOME REAL FANCY SKATING!!
RIP!
EEP!
WHAP!

BETTY! ARE YOU HURT? LET ME HELP YOU UP!
ARCHIE ANDREWS!! DON'T YOU DARE!!
?
4

REGGIE! MAY I BORROW YOUR JACKET?
FEELING A DRAFT, DOLL?
NOT NOW, THANKS TO YOUR ASSISTANCE!
TOUGH BREAK, BETTY!
WELL, THAT'S THE WAY THE SLACKS SPLIT!
GOSH! EVERYTHING'S FALLING APART TODAY! LOOK! HOW DID YOUR JACKET GET RIPPED?
WHAT'S THE DIFFERENCE, SWEETIE! LET'S SKATE!
HMMM!
6
NOW, I'LL BE...
I KNOW I HEARD SOMETHING RIP.!!
The END

Script: Frank Doyle / Pencils: Dan DeCarlo / Inks: Rudy Lapick / Letters: Victor Gorelick

Originally printed in ARCHIE'S GIRLS BETTY & VERONICA #100, APRIL 1964

VERONICA! WHAT HAPPENED? WHERE DOES IT HURT? CAN YOU MOVE? IS IT BLEEDING?
A POX ON THIS RAMSHACKLE, DECREPIT OLD BARN OF A SCHOOL!!
WHA?
THIS OLD RAT TRAP! THIS COLLAPSING OLD RUIN OUGHT TO BE CONDEMNED!!
ARE YOU TALKING ABOUT **MY** SCHOOL?
LOOK! LOOK WHAT THAT SPLINTERED OLD DOOR, DID TO MY SKIRT!
2

SPUT! IS THAT... IS THAT WHAT BROUGHT ON THAT BLOOD CURDLING SCREAM?
EASY, MR. WEATHERBEE! REMEMBER YOUR BLOOD PRESSURE!
MISS GRUNDY IS RIGHT, SIR! YOU'RE TURNING PURPLE!
BESIDES, ..IT'S NOT REALLY VERONICA'S FAULT!
WHAT?
SHE JUST CAN'T HELP BEING THE WAY SHE IS! SHE'S DIFFERENT FROM THE REST OF US!
AFTER ALL, SHE'S JUST A TYPICAL SPOILED, MADCAP HEIRESS!
3

WELL, SHE'D BETTER NOT DO ANYMORE MAD CAPPING AROUND HERE!!
SOME NERVE! INSULTING MY SCHOOL OVER A TORN SKIRT!
YOU SHOULD CONTROL YOUR TEMPER, RONNIE! MR. WEATHERBEE CAN'T HELP IT IF THE SCHOOL IS A BIT RUN DOWN!
A BIT? HAH!
ALL RIGHT, CLASS! TAKE YOUR SEATS AND LET ME HAVE YOUR ATTENTION!
I'LL SUE!! SO HELP ME! I'LL SUE THE BOARD OF EDUCATION!!
I'VE RUINED ANOTHER PAIR OF NYLONS ON THIS ROTTING OLD DESK!
4

IT'S THE MADCAP HEIRESS, MR. WEATHERBEE WITH ANOTHER COMPLAINT!
AS THE DAUGHTER OF A VERY HEAVY TAXPAYER, I **DEMAND** A NEW DESK!
I'D BE **GLAD** TO GET YOU A NEW DESK!
WE COULD USE A **THOUSAND** NEW DESKS! BUT WE CAN'T AFFORD THEM!
I CAN! I'LL BUY MY OWN!
NOW VERONICA! YOU CAN'T...
NO, NO, MISS GRUNDY! LET HER DO IT IF SHE INSISTS!
!?
ONE TAXPAYER BUYING **ONE** DESK IS A BEGINNING! MAYBE IT'LL START A **TREND**!
5

I'LL HAVE IT CHANGED TONIGHT! I WON'T SIT IN THAT EGG CRATE ANOTHER DAY!
YOU DO THAT VERONICA!
IT'LL BE A PLEASURE TO SEE SOMETHING NEW AROUND HERE!
NEXT DAY
I'VE JUST GOT TO GO IN AND SEE THAT BRIGHT, SHINY NEW DESK!
WELL, MISS GRUNDY, DID YOUR MADCAP HEIRESS SPRUCE UP YOUR ROOM A BIT?
OH, THAT SHE DID, SIR!
BUT IF IT STARTS A TREND, WE'LL NEED LARGER ROOMS!
MISS LODGE
6
The END

Script: Frank Doyle / Pencils: Dan DeCarlo / Inks: Rudy Lapick / Letters: Bill Yoshida

Originally printed in ARCHIE'S GIRLS BETTY & VERONICA #101, MAY 1964

WELL, LET'S GO HOME!
NO! NOW MY CURIOSITY IS AROUSED!
SH
I'VE GOT TO SEE WHAT HE'S WORKING ON IN THERE!
SHOP
WELL, NOW YOU KNOW WHAT HE'S WORKING ON IN THERE!
SHOP
A GIRL WOODWORKER? WHO IS SHE KIDDING?!
HER DAD IS A CABINET MAKER! SHE'S VERY GOOD WITH TOOLS!
UNFORTUNATELY, SHE'S NOT BAD WITHOUT TOOLS!
2

IN ONE WAY IT'S FUNNY, THOUGH!
ARCHIE CAN'T EVEN SAW A STRAIGHT LINE!
WHEN IT COMES TO CHISELING, THOUGH, HE HAS NO EQUAL!
NEXT DAY:
ARE YOU SURE YOU DON'T HAVE A GIRL FRIEND OR TWO ON THE STRING?
WOULD I LIE TO YOU, DARLING?
WHY UNTIL I MET YOU, I DIDN'T EVEN KNOW WOMEN EXISTED!
ARCHIE! YOU'RE SWEET!
SHOP
NO GIRL AT ALL BEFORE ME, EH!
NARY A ONE!
THEN WHAT DOES THIS "V" IN A HEART STAND FOR ON YOUR PROJECT?
ULP!
3

ER-AH-VICTORY, OF COURSE! IT MEANS, I **LOVE** VICTORY!
IT'S A MISERABLE JOB OF CARVING!
LOOK, YOU'VE GOT TO HOLD THE TOOL THUSLY AND...
TOOL, SCHMOOL! LET'S TALK ABOUT US!
WHY DON'T WE BUILD A LITTLE ROMANCE TOGETHER, AND...
CRASH!
WHY THE HECK DIDN'T YOU WARN ME ABOUT THAT WEAK BOARD?
IT WASN'T SUPPOSED TO BE WEAK!
LOOK! IT WAS **SAWED** ALMOST IN **TWO**!
I COULD HAVE BROKEN MY NECK!
4

NOW, LET'S GO TO WORK BEFORE WE SAY SOMETHING WERE SORRY FOR!
ALL RIGHT, LOVER! I'M SORRY!
GET ME THE VARNISH, WILL YOU? I'VE GOT TO PUT THE FINAL COAT ON THIS BOOKCASE OF MINE!
HERE YOU ARE, ANGEL!
EEYIPE!!
THE VARNISH IS FULL OF SAND!!
YOU IDIOT! YOU RUINED MY TOP!
DON'T CALL ME AN IDIOT!!
...AND YOUR TOP WAS RUINED LONG BEFORE I CAME ALONG!
5

THAT DOES IT! I'M THROUGH WITH...
WATCH THAT HAM...
OOOWWW!
MY TOE!
CLICK!
CLUNK
OOOW!
WHRRRRRRRR
EEEEOOOOOW!
SO ARCHIE QUIT THE WOODWORKING GAME, EH?
YES! HE CUT OUT!
6
...(GIGGLE) COULDN'T STAND THE GRIND!
?
The END

Script: Frank Doyle / Pencils: Dan DeCarlo / Inks: Rudy Lapick / Letters: Vince DeCarlo

Originally printed in ARCHIE'S GIRLS BETTY & VERONICA #105, SEPTEMBER 1964

THE TAJ MAHAL! NOW THATS PRETTY JAZZY!
MAKE A FABULOUS DRIVE-IN!
THERE'S A WEIRD MONSTROSITY!
YOU'D THINK THE FRENCH COULD COVER IT WITH SOMETHING!
I YEARN FOR THE SOUTHERN SUN, DARLING! SHALL WE DRIFT DOWN INTO SPAIN?
LEAVE US!
SPAIN! WE SAID SPAIN!
WHAT KIND OF TRAVEL AGENT ARE YOU!
SORRY, LADIES! THE MECHANISM IS JAMMED, OR THERE'S A SHORT OR SOMETHING!
EIFFEL TOWER
TAJ MAHAL
2

THEY ARE BEAUTIFUL SCENIC BACKDROPS, THOUGH!
IT'S A COOL GADGET, ISN'T IT?
THE TRAVEL CLUB RENTED IT FOR THIS YEARS PAGEANT OF ALL NATIONS!
IT MAKES YOU WANT TO GO, DOESN'T IT?
MAYBE WE CAN ARRANGE A LITTLE TRIP SOMEWHERE THIS AFTERNOON!
I'D BETTER STAY AND FIX THIS!
A TRIP? NOW?
WE JUST FEEL LIKE GOING SOMEWHERE! SEEING SOMETHING!
BETTY! CALL HOME AND TELL YOUR MOTHER YOU'LL BE LATE FOR DINNER!
WE'RE GOING SOMEPLACE?
EVERYPLACE! YOU'RE TAKING A TRIP AROUND THE WORLD!
HUH?
3

WE'RE MAKING THE FINAL TEST ON OUR NEW EXPERIMENTAL SHIP TODAY!
THERE'S NO REASON WHY YOU TWO CAN'T REPLACE SOME OF THE CARGO!
YOU MEAN WE'RE ACTUALLY GOING AROUND THE WORLD?
LODGE AERONAUTICS
NO
JUST RELAX, ENJOY YOURSELVES AND GIVE ME YOUR OPINION OF THE SHIP WHEN YOU RETURN!
XL 7
GOLLEE!
GERMANY, RUSSIA, CHINA, JAPAN, INDIA...WOW! I'VE ALWAYS WANTED TO SEE THOSE PLACES!
ISN'T DADDY A LOVABLE OLD BEAR? HE'S ALWAYS THERE WHEN YOU NEED HIM!
4

CAPTAIN! WILL WE BE STARTING SOON?
STARTING, MISS LODGE?
...WE'RE PASSING OVER ENGLAND AT THE MOMENT!
WHAT?
DO NOT TALK TO PILOTS
HE'S RIGHT! WE'RE IN THE AIR!
BUT WHERE'S ENGLAND?
XL7
CAPTAIN! WE DON'T SEE ENGLAND!
NO, MISS LODGE!
WE'RE OVER RUSSIA, NOW!
TEL SC5
BUT IN ANY EVENT, WE'RE TOO HIGH AND TOO FAST TO SEE ANYTHING!
5

I CAN SEE MORE OF THE WORLD WALKING DOWN TO THE DELICATESSEN!
THIS IS PROGRESS?
THERE GOES JAPAN, LADIES!
BIG DEAL!
SAYONARA!
AH! HOME AGAIN, SAME DAY! DID YOU HAVE A GOOD TRIP?
OH, GREAT! JUST GREAT!
YOU DON'T SOUND VERY ENTHUSIASTIC!
YOU KNOW WHY, DADDY? BECAUSE WE'RE NOT!
INGRATES! THAT'S WHAT YOU ARE? I GAVE YOU A TRIP COMPLETELY AROUND THE WORLD!
WHAT MORE DO YOU WANT?
WE'D LIKE TO GO SOMEWHERE ELSE!
The END

Script: Frank Doyle / Pencils: Dan DeCarlo / Inks: Rudy Lapick / Letters: Vince DeCarlo

Originally printed in ARCHIE'S GIRLS BETTY & VERONICA #106, OCTOBER 1964

SAY, I HEAR YOU DID PRETTY WELL TODAY, ARCHIE!
MAN! DID I EVER, STAN!!
THEY WERE BITING LIKE IT WAS GOING OUT OF STYLE!
I'LL HAVE TO TRY THAT SPOT!
ARCHIE! WHO IS THAT GORGEOUS CREATURE?
WHO, WHO, WHO?
STAN? HE'S JUST THE GUY WHO RENTS THE BOATS DOWN AT THE LAKE!
NEXT DAY:
ALL SET?
YOU KNOW IT, GIRL!
ISN'T IT WONDERFUL, HOW QUICKLY WE PICKED UP THIS NEW HOBBY?
THERE'S NOTHING NEW ABOUT THIS HOBBY, BETTY!
2

DO YOU GIRLS WANT A BOAT?
NOT REALLY, BUT I GUESS WE'D BETTER TAKE ONE!
GIGGLE
LEE'S BOATS
LOTS OF LUCK! HOPE YOU FIND A GOOD FISHING SPOT!
THANKS, HANDSOME!
WE'VE GOT A REAL PRIME SPOT ALL PICKED OUT!
ROAR!
...AND THIS IS IT!
PERFECT!
PUTT PUTT SPUT!
BEST LIL' OL' FISHING SPOT ON THE LAKE, EH, BETTY?
OH IT'S A DAN-DAN-DANDY!
?
LEE'S
3

YOU GIRLS WILL NEVER GET A BITE THAT CLOSE TO SHORE!
WE'LL TAKE OUR CHANCES!
MAYBE WE'RE NOT FISHING FOR THE SAME THINGS OTHER PEOPLE FISH FOR!
WHOOPS!!
OF ALL THE DAD-RATTED STUPID LUCK! I GOT A BITE!!
MAN, WHAT A MONSTER! HE'S TOO BIG FOR THE LINE!
SNAP!
4

TOUGH LUCK, GIRLS!
IS HE KIDDING?
CHARLIE! TAKE OVER THE BOATS FOR A WHILE, WILL YOU?
HE'S HOOKED!
NOW THAT YOU'RE OFF DUTY, STAN, WHAT SHALL WE DO?
BAIT UP, OF COURSE!
IF WE'RE LUCKY WE MIGHT GET A SECOND CHANCE AT THAT BIG BABY!
SAY, DID I HEAR RIGHT? DID YOU TWO GO FISHING THIS MORNING?
NOW THERE'S AN ODDBALL IDEA!
FISHING? YECH!
5
CAN YOU IMAGINE US INDULGING IN SUCH A SILLY PASTIME?
NEVER IN A MILLION YEARS!
The END

Script: George Gladir / Pencils: Dan DeCarlo / Inks: Rudy Lapick / Letters: Vince DeCarlo

Originally printed in ARCHIE'S GIRLS BETTY & VERONICA #109, JANUARY 1965

WHAT YOU CAN DO FOR BETTY, YOU CAN DO FOR ME!
I WANT TO WEAR A GLAMOROUS UNIFORM IN YOUR PLAY!
BUT, BABY DOLL...
...YOU'RE NOT EVEN IN THE DRAMA CLUB!
ARE YOU GOING TO SPLIT HAIRS?
(GULP) I'M NOT EVEN GOING TO QUIBBLE!
JUG! FIX THIS GAL UP WITH COSTUME NUMBER THIRTY-THREE!
DRESSING ROOM
HERE YOU ARE! THE DRESSING ROOM IS OVER THERE!
THANK YOU!
33

OKAY, REG! PUT ON YOUR HEAD AND RUN THROUGH YOUR ROUTINE!
RIGHT, CHIEF!
ALL RIGHT! YOU HAD YOUR LAUGH!
PEANUTS
PEANUTS
YOU ASKED FOR A UNIFORM!
YOU ASKED FOR A FAT LIP!
PEANUTS
SHE WANTS A MORE IMPORTANT ROLL, JUG! TRY COSTUME NUMBER TWENTY-SEVEN!
CHECK!
PEANUTS
PEANUTS
I DON'T THINK SHE'S GOING TO CARE FOR IT, ARCH!
IT'S ALL I'VE GOT FOR HER!
MY! YOU'RE A REAL BARREL OF LAUGHS, TODAY, ARCHIE ANDREWS!
3

WHOOPS! SORRY I'M LATE FOR THE REHEARSAL!
YOWTCH!
WAP!
YOU FORGOT TO WEAR YOUR PADDING?
HOW DID YOU GUESS?
I'LL GET EVEN! I'LL RUIN HIS WHOLE SHOW!
DRESSING ROOM
MAN! IT'S HOT IN THIS SUIT!
DRESSING ROOM
REGGIE, DARLING! I HAVE A WONDERFUL SUGGESTION!
YOU **DO**?
4

OKAY! LET'S GET BACK TO WORK! GET THAT CAT OUT HERE!
SNAP! SNAP!
WHOA, SIMBA! EASY BOY! SIT! I SAID SIT!
SNAP
DON'T BE A WISE GUY, REGGIE! DO THE BALANCING BALL BIT!
COME OFF IT, REGGIE! THIS ISN'T A COMEDY ROUTINE!
5

THAT ALSO ISN'T REGGIE! HE'S OUT AT THE COKE MACHINE!
NOW PRETEND TO ATTACK THE LION TAMER! MAKE IT LOOK REAL, FEROCIOUS, DANGEROUS!
HOW'S THIS, CHIEF! HEE, HEE!
VERONICA!
ON GUARD PUSSY CAT! I'VE BEEN PRACTICING FOR THIS PART!
(SIGH) SOMETIMES, MISS GRUNDY, I WONDER WHAT WE'RE RUNNING HERE!
CRACK!
YOWL!
OUCH!
YIPE!
6
The END

Script: George Gladir / Pencils: Dan DeCarlo / Inks: Rudy Lapick / Letters: Vince DeCarlo

Originally printed in ARCHIE'S GIRLS BETTY & VERONICA #109, JANUARY 1965

IT'S A CLOTHES CLEANER, SIR! IF IT WORKS WE'LL MAKE MILLIONS!
CHEMISTRY
..NOT THAT VERONICA NEEDS MILLIONS!
IT'S THE THRILL OF SUCCESS THAT COUNTS!
WELL, HAVE FUN, AND DON'T BLOW UP THE LAB!
DO YOU THINK THAT'S IT?
I'D LIKE TO TRY IT!
HI, GIRLS! HOW...
LET'S SEE THAT SWEATSHIRT, ARCHIE!
HEY! THAT'S INK!
YOU'RE BRILLIANT TODAY, SON!
2

NOW DON'T GET IN A FLAP ABOUT IT! EVERYTHING WILL BE ALL RIGHT!
...WE HOPE!
HEY! THE SPOT'S GONE! IT'S **CLEAN**!
IT WORKS!!
BY GOLLY, THEY'VE GOT A GOOD THING GOING HERE!
GYM
LOOK AT THAT! JUST LOOK AT THAT MESS!
WHAT HAPPENED MR. WEATHERBEE, SIR?
I'VE GOT STAINS ALL OVER MY SUIT!
3

I WAS CHANGING, TO HAVE A LITTLE WORKOUT! THERE WAS GREASE ON THE LOCKER WALL!
HEY! BETTY AND VERONICAS' NEW CLEANER WILL FIX THAT IN A JIFFY!
YOU MEAN IT **WORKS?**
IT TOOK AN INK STAIN OUT OF MY SWEATSHIRT IN ONE MINUTE!
WHY, THAT'S GREAT!
..AND THE CLOTHES DRY ALMOST IMMEDIATELY!
GIVE THEM MY SUIT!
WORD OF OUR SUCCESS IS SPREADING!
BY TOMORROW THERE'LL BE A **PRICE** ON THIS SERVICE!
BEAUTIFUL JOB!
4

WITH MR. WEATHERBEE PLUGGING OUR CLEANER WE'RE OFF TO A GOOD START!
CHEMISTRY
WE'LL HAVE TO DESIGN A NICE CONTAINER! PACKAGING IS SO IMPORTANT!
DISTRIBUTION! EVENTUALLY WE'LL GO WORLD WIDE!
BUT OF COURSE!
THE PRODUCT ITSELF DOESN'T SEEM TO HAVE ANY FLAWS THAT I CAN SEE!
I CAN'T SEE ANYTHING THAT ANYONE WOULD OBJECT TO!
ER- PERHAPS I MIGHT SUGGEST ONE SMALL POSSIBILITY?
CHEMISTRY
5
The END

Script: Frank Doyle / Pencils: Dan DeCarlo / Inks: Rudy Lapick

Originally printed in ARCHIE'S GIRLS BETTY & VERONICA #111, MARCH 1965

WELL,..IF YOU WANT TO CONFESS YOUR INDISCRETIONS...
IT WASN'T AN INDISCRETION!
IT WAS AN INNOCENT MOVIE WITH BETTY! THAT'S NO SIN!!
THEN WHY ARE YOU SO APOLOGETIC?
I AM NOT APOLOGETIC!!
YOU'RE JEALOUS! YOU'RE VINDICTIVE, VENGEFUL AND POSSESSIVE!... AND YOU EMPTIED THAT PITCHER ON ME ON PURPOSE!
HEY!
I JUST HAD WORDS WITH VERONICA, THE ACCIDENT ARRANGER!
7
2

SEE ?
SHE ARRANGED THAT ?
JUST BECAUSE I TOOK YOU TO A MOVIE!
WHY DID YOU SET YOUR LITTLE FRIENDS ON POOR ARCHIE ?
HUH ?
YOU'RE JEALOUS, VINDICTIVE, VENGEFUL!
YOU FORGOT "POSSESSIVE!"
HMPH!
WHOOPS!
3

HOW JEALOUS CAN YOU **GET**?
YOU OUGHT TO BE ASHAMED OF YOURSELF!
DADDY! I DIDN'T DO ANYTHING?
DON'T DENY IT, DAUGHTER! I KNOW YOU TOO WELL!
SHE'S A DANGEROUS WOMAN TO CROSS!
CRASH!
KLUNK!
EGAD! EVEN HER OWN FATHER ISN'T SAFE!!

BEAT IT! IT WENT THROUGH MR. LODGE'S WINDOW!
WELL, HOW'M I DOIN'?
(GULP)- WHO ARE **YOU**?
YOUR FAIRY GODMOTHER, DEARIE! I'M PROTECTING YOUR INTERESTS!
I MADE YOU EMPTY THAT PITCHER ON ARCHIE AND CAUSED A WAGON TO RUN HIM DOWN!
SLURP!
...I ARRANGED FOR BETTY TO TRIP ON THE HOSE AND I JUST CLUNKED DEAR OL' DAD WITH A BASEBALL!
WHAT ARE YOU, SOME KIND OF NUT?
!?
5

I CAN HANDLE MY OWN PROBLEMS WITHOUT ANY HOKUS POKUS!!
YOU'RE AN INTERFERING OLD BUSYBODY AND I WISH YOU'D LEAVE ME ALONE!
WHOOPS!
EEP!
IF THERE'S ONE THING I CAN'T STAND, IT'S INGRATITUDE!
6
The END

Script: Frank Doyle / Art: Dan DeCarlo

Originally printed in ARCHIE'S GIRLS BETTY & VERONICA #112, APRIL 1965

THIS SLOBBERING CAN OF SARDINES CAN BOW AND KISS HANDS?
NOT THE FISH! THE PROFESSOR!
HE'D SOONER SPIT IN YOUR EYE THAN LOOK AT YOU!
PROFESSOR FLUTESNOOT?
NO! THE FISH!
THESE SPOUTERS ARE VERY RARE! THEY COST QUITE A BIT OF MONEY!
REALLY?
MAYBE THERE'S MORE TO THIS THAN MEETS THE EYE!
SCIENCE
SPLAT!
2

THAT MOLDY MACKEREL! I OUGHT TO SEW UP HIS GILLS!
WHAT HAPPENED?
SCIENCE
THAT ILL MANNERED FISH JUST SPIT IN MY FACE!
HE'S LONELY! HE NEEDS COMPANY!
FACULTY LOUNGE
HERE! WE'LL TAKE THIS SPLIT-TAIL OUT OF THE COMMUNITY TANK! HE'S A REAL FRIENDLY FISH!
FACULTY LOUNGE
NOW WE'LL GO BACK TO THE SCIENCE ROOM AND PUT HIM IN WITH YOUR FRIEND!
HE'S NO FRIEND OF MINE!
DO I JUST DUMP HIM IN?
POUR AWAY, GIRL!
THANKS VERY MUCH, JUGGIE! YOU'VE DONE YOUR GOOD DEED FOR TODAY!
OH, I'M A GOOD OL' SCOUT!
3

THAT SPLIT-TAIL IS A GREAT LITTLE FISH FOR KEEPING OTHER FISH HAPPY!
THAT'S NICE!
... EXCEPT, OF COURSE, FOR SPOUTER FISH!
HUH?
MY, YES! A SPLIT-TAIL WILL GOBBLE UP A SPOUTER FASTER THAN YOU CAN SAY HOLY MACKEREL!
HOLY MACKEREL!
BUT YOU WON'T CATCH OL' FLUTE-SNOOT LAYING OUT THE MONEY, IT COSTS TO BUY A SPOUTER! NO, SIR! YOU WON'T SEE ONE OF THOSE AROUND HERE!
(GULP)-NOT ANYMORE, ANYWAY!
SCIENCE
PLEASE! BE THERE! SQUIRT! PLEASE! JUST ONE LITTLE SQUIRT!!
4

SOMETHING WRONG, BETTY?
(SNIFF) YOUR SPOUTER, SIR! YOUR EXPENSIVE SPOUTER! HE'S GONE!
SCIENCE
YES! I MOVED HIM TO THE COMMUNITY TANK A WHILE AGO!
SCIENCE
SOMEBODY HAD TAKEN THAT VICIOUS SPLIT-TAIL OUT!
MY SPOUTER IS AS HAPPY AS THE HALIBUT NOW THAT HE'S IN WITH ALL THOSE FRIENDLY FISH!
?
BETTY! WHAT IN THE WORLD ARE YOU DOING?
WELCOMING BACK AN OLD FRIEND!
FACULTY LOUNGE
SPLAT!
The END

Script: Frank Doyle / Art: Dan DeCarlo

Originally printed in ARCHIE'S GIRLS BETTY & VERONICA #113, MAY 1965

WELL, PERHAPS A LITTLE HARD WORK WILL STEM THE FLOW OF CHATTER!
BOOK
MISS MARIAN WOULD LIKE THESE OLD BOOKS TAKEN DOWN TO THE STOREROOM!
YOU WANT US, ...US FRAIL FEMALES TO MOVE ALL THOSE HEAVY BOOKS?
HERE! USE THIS CART!
NOW START LOADING!
HEY! LOOK WHO'S BEEN PUT TO WORK!
LIBRARY
OOF!
GRUNT!
PUFF!
2

WHEW! I'VE GOT TO REST! HOW COME THIS HALLWAY SEEMS SO **UPHILL**?
YIPES!
BECAUSE IT **IS**!
HELP!
SOMEBODY STOP IT!!
OOPS
MY THE SIGHTS YOU SEE WHEN YOU DON'T HAVE YOUR CAMERA!
3

NICE TRY, MISS GRUNDY!
WHO WAS TRYING?
IT'S NOT OUR FAULT THAT THIS OLD SCHOOL TILTS!
JUST HANG ON THIS TIME!
I THOUGHT SHE TOOK IT VERY CALMLY!
SHE WAS STILL IN SHOCK!
MADE IT!
FINALLY! LET'S GET RID OF THIS LOAD!
STORAGE
AH! IT ROLLS SO EASILY WHEN IT'S EMPTY!
STORAGE
4

SAY! DO YOU REALIZE THAT IT'S **DOWNHILL** BACK TO THE LIBRARY?
SO WE JUST WON'T LET GO OF THE CART!
THAT ISN'T WHAT I HAD IN MIND!
WHY SHOULDN'T WE **RIDE** THIS STAGECOACH BACK TO THE WAY STATION!
(GIGGLE) DO WE DARE?
I THINK WE CAN STEER IT BY LEANING!
CAST OFF! I'LL NAVIGATE!
HEADS UP!
RIDE 'EM COWBOY!
Z-OOM!
5

NICE TURN.!
I WONDER HOW WE STOP THIS THING.!
SCREEEEE
NOW THAT ALL THOSE OLD BOOKS ARE OUT OF HERE, MY LIBRARY IS SO NEAT AND CLEAN AGAIN.!
LIBRA
WATCH IT!!
WAP!
WHAT DID I DO TO DESERVE THOSE **TWO**?
THIS IS JUST THE SCRUB TEAM, MISS MARIAN.!
TOMORROW YOU GET ARCHIE AND JUGHEAD.!
The END
6

Script: Frank Doyle / Pencils: Dan DeCarlo / Inks & Letters: Vince DeCarlo

Originally printed in ARCHIE'S GIRLS BETTY & VERONICA #118, OCTOBER 1965

NOW, NOW, GIRLS! YOU SHOULDN'T FIGHT OVER THE GAME!
YOU KNOW YOU CAN'T VAULT THAT NET! WHY DO YOU ALWAYS TRY?
IT'S TRADITION!
SHEEP! THAT'S WHAT YOU ARE! MUST YOU ALWAYS CONFORM TO TRADITION?
IF IT WAS TRADITION TO STAND ON YOUR HEAD WHEN A BOY CAME ALONG, YOU'D...
HI, GIRLS!
WHAT'S WITH YOU, BETTY?
2

DUMMY! I SAID IF IT WAS TRADITION!
I GOT CARRIED AWAY!
YOU SHOULD BE! BY THE MEN IN THE WHITE COATS!
WHAT'S THE BEEF?
SHE'S GOT NO INDIVIDUALITY!
SHE FOLLOWS RULES LIKE A WELL TRAINED DOG!
RULES ARE RULES!
RULES, MY GIRL, ARE MADE TO BE BROKEN!
IF THEY'RE MADE TO BE BROKEN WHY MAKE THEM IN THE FIRST PLACE?
3

WELL, HOW DO YOU LIKE THAT? WE'RE ACTUALLY ALONE!
YEAH! HOW ABOUT THAT?
DO YOU INCLUDE RULES OF FAIR PLAY AND STUFF LIKE THAT?
ALL RULES, CHILD! THE ONLY WAY TO SUCCESS IS TO MAKE YOUR OWN RULES!
SHE'LL NEVER SUCCEED! TO MUCH GOODY-GOODY!
NOW, WHERE WERE WE?
DID YOUR DAD MAKE HIS MILLIONS BY BREAKING RULES?
SMASHED THEM TO PIECES!
4

IN THIS LIFE YOU'VE GOT TO BE RUTHLESS! NO HOLDS BARRED!
YOU WANT SOMETHING, YOU GO AHEAD AND GET IT! ... ANYWAY AT ALL!
VERONICA!
YOUR DAD WANTS YOU IMMEDIATELY!
OH, DEAR! I'VE GOT TO GO!
DID I DO, OKAY, BETTY?
FINE, TIMMY! HERE'S YOUR QUARTER!
5
YOU LEARN FAST!
HAD A GOOD TEACHER!
The END

Script: Jim Ruth / Pencils: Dan DeCarlo / Inks & Letters: Vince DeCarlo

Originally printed in ARCHIE'S GIRLS BETTY & VERONICA #118, OCTOBER 1965

ARCHIE, I'M ALL WET!
NEW OUTFIT, BETTY? IT LOOKS POSITIVELY FLASHY, OR IS IT SPLASHY?
THAT'S NOT FUNNY! I WAS JUST TELLING ARCHIE ABOUT THE VACATION I'D LIKE, WITH THE OCEAN SPRAY IN MY FACE....
AND I WAS STANDING RIGHT HERE!
BETTY...
AND THEN ALONG CAME A...
SPLASH!
2

LOOK!!
IT HAPPENED AGAIN!
IF YOU'RE GOING TO DO ANYMORE DAY DREAMING, BETTY, MAYBE YOU'D BETTER WEAR A RAINCOAT!
WHY DON'T YOU THINK OF TWO WEEKS IN THE GOBI DESERT... THEN MAYBE YOU'D DRY OFF!
RONNIE, WHY WERE YOU SO NASTY TO POOR BETTY?
ME?!
YOU'RE THE ONE WHO'S GETTING NASTY! WHY ALL I SAID WAS...
YOU KNOW... HE'S RIGHT?!
3

LATER...
GEE, I FEEL, BAD ABOUT WHAT I SAID TO BETTY! BUT I DIDN'T MEAN IT!
MIRROR, MIRROR ON THE WALL, TELL ME WHO IS THE NASTIEST...I MEAN MOST BEAUTIFUL OF ALL!
FIRST THINGS FIRST, **YOU** ARE THE **NASTIEST!!**
I MUST BE FLIPPING!
I'M THE ONE WHO NEEDS A VACATION!
I'LL SHOW THAT OLD MIRROR! I'LL **TAKE** BETTY WITH ME!
4

BETTY, YOU'RE GOING ON A VACATION WITH ME, AND I WON'T TAKE NO FOR AN ANSWER!
WOW! I'LL BE PACKED IN A MINUTE!
I TAKE IT ALL BACK, RONNIE, YOU'RE NOT NASTY AT ALL!
SO LONG, GIRLS, HAVE FUN!
AND SO...
THIS IS GREAT, RONNIE, I CAN ALMOST FEEL THE OCEAN SPRAY NOW!
SPLASH!
SPEEDBALL
THE END

Script: Frank Doyle / Pencils: Dan DeCarlo / Inks: Rudy Lapick / Letters: Bill Yoshida

Originally printed in ARCHIE'S GIRLS BETTY & VERONICA #120, DECEMBER 1965

HOLD STILL! I'LL HAVE YOU FREE IN A MINUTE!
TAKE YOUR TIME!
AHA!
!?
AHA?
AHA!!
THAT'S A FINE WAY TO KEEP A DATE WITH ME!
VERONICA GOT CAUGHT!
HA! SOMEBODY GOT CAUGHT, BUT IT WASN'T VERONICA!
GOLLY! SHE'S ANGRY!
THERE, YOU'RE FREE!
2

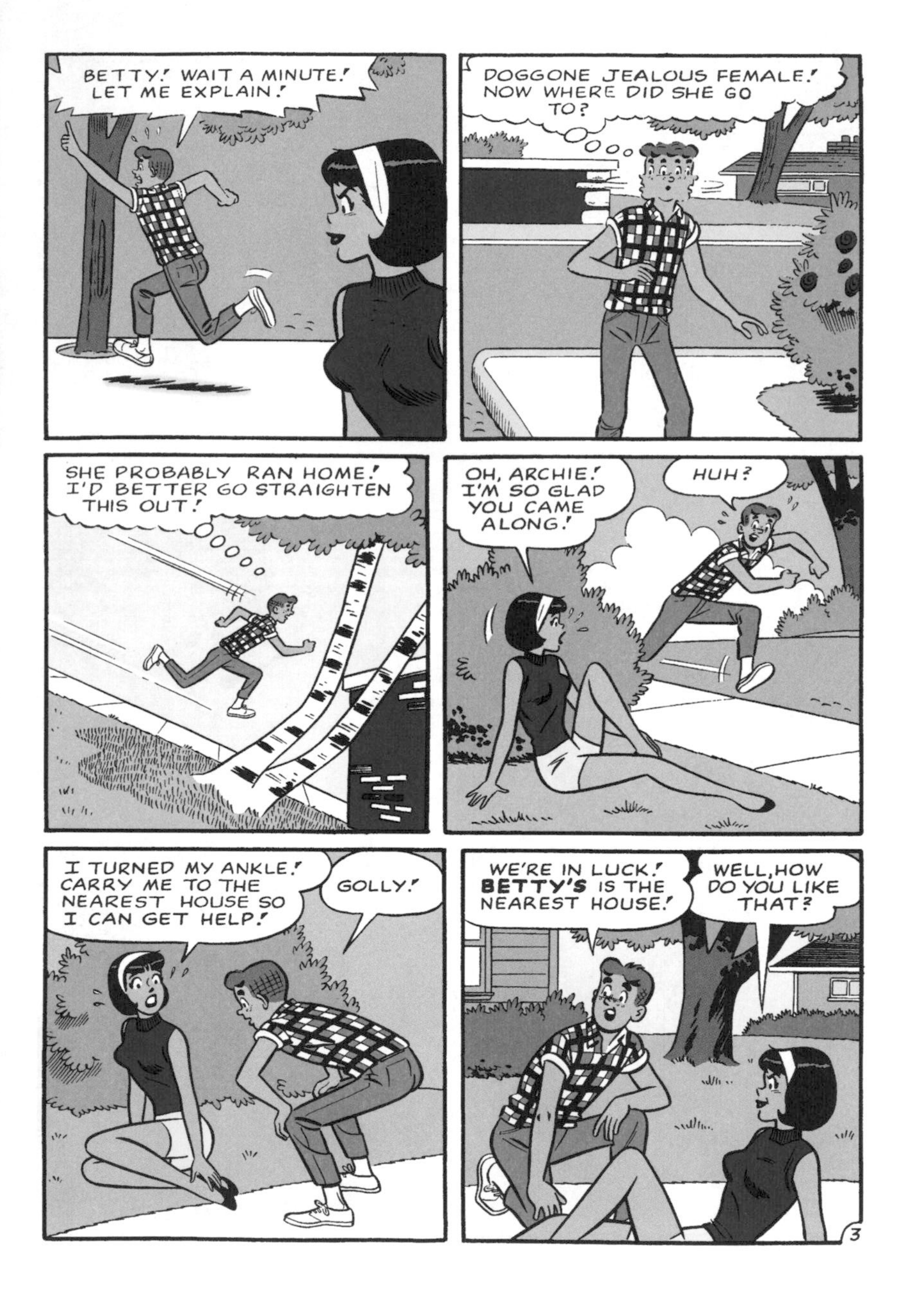
BETTY! WAIT A MINUTE! LET ME EXPLAIN!
DOGGONE JEALOUS FEMALE! NOW WHERE DID SHE GO TO?
SHE PROBABLY RAN HOME! I'D BETTER GO STRAIGHTEN THIS OUT!
OH, ARCHIE! I'M SO GLAD YOU CAME ALONG!
HUH?
I TURNED MY ANKLE! CARRY ME TO THE NEAREST HOUSE SO I CAN GET HELP!
GOLLY!
WE'RE IN LUCK! **BETTY'S** IS THE NEAREST HOUSE!
WELL, HOW DO YOU LIKE THAT?
3

I WAS COMING OVER TO STRAIGHTEN OUT THAT SILLY MISUNDER-STANDING!
OF COURSE YOU WERE!
BETTY, I HAVE SOMETHING TO EXPLAIN!
GASP!
BUT FIRST WE'D BETTER DO SOME-THING ABOUT VERONICA!
A CAPITAL IDEA!
SHE TURNED HER ANKLE JUST OUT-SIDE YOUR DOOR!
SURE SHE DID!
HAVE YOU ANY TAPE? WE SHOULD TAPE THAT ANKLE TIGHTLY!
BUT OF COURSE!
ARE YOU SURE YOU DIDN'T TWIST YOUR **NECK** A LITTLE BIT, TOO?
YOU WOULDN'T DARE!
4

THAT'S FINE! NOW I'LL LIMP HOME AND GET OUT OF YOUR WAY!
ARE YOU SURE YOU CAN MAKE IT?
WELL, PERHAPS YOU'D BETTER SEE ME AS FAR AS MY DOOR!
WHAT ELSE?
I'LL BE RIGHT BACK, BETTY!
I'LL BET!
OH, ARCHIE! YOU'RE SO STRONG! HOW CAN I EVER THANK YOU?
AW! IT'S NOTHING, RON! I...
HEADS UP!
RROARR!!
WAP!
5

OH, WHAT A SHAME! THE POOR BOY IS HURT!
I'LL TAKE CARE OF HIM!
NONSENSE! YOU HOBBLE HOME AND HAVE A DOCTOR LOOK AT THAT ANKLE!
I'LL TAKE CARE OF THIS GOOD SAMARITAN HERE!
TOODLE, DARLING! HAVE A HAPPY RECOVERY!
CRAZY FEMALE! PAYS US TO SMEAR HIM AND THEN TAKES HIM HOME WITH HER!
GIRLS DON'T MAKE SENSE!
NO, BUT THEY SURE MAKE TROUBLE!
6
The END

Script: Frank Doyle / Pencils: Dan DeCarlo / Inks: Rudy Lapick / Letters: Vince DeCarlo

Originally printed in ARCHIE'S GIRLS BETTY & VERONICA #124, APRIL 1966

SHE THREATENED ME WITH REGGIE! SHE WANTS TO MAKE ME JEALOUS!
FIRE, SHOULD BE FOUGHT WITH FIRE!
...YOU MAKE HER JEALOUS!
SMERP!
WHEW! LAY OFF BEFORE YOU MELT ALL THE SNOW!
LET'S MOVE OFF NOW, AND LET HER MAKE THE NEXT MOVE!
HOW DARE HE? HOW DARE HE STEAL MY THUNDER LIKE THAT?
2

REGGIE? HELLO! YES, I WANT TO SPEAK TO REGGIE!!
GULP! HE'S NOT HOME?
SOMETHING IS UPSETTING MY LITTLE BABY?
CRASH!
I'VE GOT TO DO A LOATHESOME THING, DADDY!
AGAIN?
I'VE GOT TO BUTTER UP, ... SMOOTH TALK, .. SNUGGLE UP TO THAT ARCHIE TO GET HIM BACK IN MY POWER!
SLIPPED OUT FROM UNDER THE THUMB, DID HE?
I'LL HAVE HIM BACK REAL SOON, DADDY!
3

A TIGRESS HAS GOT TO PROTECT WHAT'S HERS!
THIS STUPID BLIZZARD! I CAN BARELY **SEE!**
WE'D BETTER HEAD HOME, BETTY! THE SNOW IS TOO HEAVY!
"SNOW"? WHAT SNOW?
SEE YOU TOMORROW, BETTY!
'BYE, ARCHIEKINS!
SOUP
(SIGH) IT WAS FUN WHILE IT LASTED!
AHA!
4

LOOK AT THEM CUDDLING UP! IT'S REVOLTING!
GLORY BE! SHE'S GOING! SHE'S ACTUALLY GOING OFF AND LEAVING HIM UNPROTECTED!
WELL, I HATE TO DO THIS, BUT I'VE GOT TO MAKE HIM THINK HE WON THIS ROUND!
DARLING! FORGIVE ME! I'VE TREATED YOU MISERABLY! SHALL WE FORGET ALL...
TSK, TSK! JUST LOOK AT THAT! THE THINGS SOME PEOPLE THROW AWAY!
THE END
5

Script: Frank Doyle / Pencils: Dan DeCarlo / Inks: Rudy Lapick / Letters: Vince DeCarlo

Originally printed in ARCHIE'S GIRLS BETTY & VERONICA #126, JUNE 1966

YOU'RE REALLY CRAZY ABOUT THAT CAR, AREN'T YOU?
I SURE AM!
YOU'RE MY LITTLE SWEETHEART, AREN'T YOU?
PAT PAT
MATTER OF FACT, I LOVE YOU, I DO!
SMACK!
HOW COULD HE DO THIS TO ME! WELL, I'D BETTER BREAK THIS UP IN A HURRY!
ARCHIE!!
2

HI, RONNIE!
WHAT'S ALL THIS LOVEY DOVEY STUFF I HEAR COMING FROM THE GARAGE?
YOU REALLY CAN'T BLAME ME! BESIDES, WHEN I GET HER ALL TUNED UP YOU'LL SEE WHAT I MEAN!
OF COURSE THE CHASSIS MIGHT NEED A LITTLE WORK!
WHAT?
AND I SUPPOSE YOU'RE CRAZY ABOUT THAT DUMB OLD PONY TAIL, TOO!
WHAT'S SHE TALKING ABOUT? WHO EVER HEARD OF A CAR WITH A PONY TAIL?
THIS IS GOING TO BE TOUGHER THAN I THOUGHT! HE'S REALLY FLIPPED OVER THAT DUMB BLONDE!
3

WHAT'S WRONG, RONNIE? YOU LOOK AS MAD AS A JEALOUS FEMALE!
THAT'S JUST WHAT I AM! THE WAY HE WAS TALKING TO HER IN THE GARAGE WOULD GET YOU SICK!
CALLING HER HIS LITTLE SWEETHEART, AND SAYING HE LOVED HER... YAGGH!
Sale
35¢
WHEN I SEE HER I COULD SCRATCH HER CHEATING HEART OUT!
BETTER WATCH OUT FOR THE RADIATOR, IT'S MURDER ON YOUR FINGERNAILS!
WHAT ARE YOU TALKING ABOUT?
WHEN ARCHIE GETS THAT MUSHY IN A GARAGE HE'S GOT TO BE TALKING ABOUT HIS CAR!
4

TO THINK, ALL I'VE BEEN JEALOUS OF ALL THIS TIME WAS ARCHIE'S OLD CAR!
WAIT'LL I TELL HIM! HE'LL GET A BIG LAUGH OUT OF THIS!
ARCHIE, DO YOU WANT TO HEAR SOMETHING FUNNY?
LOOK OUT, RONNIE! DO YOU WANT TO SCRATCH MY CAR?
BOY, OF ALL THE ... THERE BABY! SHE DIDN'T HURT YOU, DID SHE?
PAT PAT
5
YOU KNOW, I HAD EVERY RIGHT TO BE JEALOUS!
The END

Script: Dick Malmgren / Pencils: Dan DeCarlo / Inks: Rudy Lapick

Originally printed in ARCHIE'S GIRLS BETTY & VERONICA #136, APRIL 1967

I THINK YOU'RE WEARING YOUR SKATES IN THE WRONG PLACE! HEH! HEH!
VERY FUNNY!
MAYBE YOU SHOULD GET A PAIR OF LEARNER'S SKATES! HA! HA! HEH! HEH!
RONNIE! SEEING YOU KNOW HOW TO SKATE SO WELL, MAYBE I OUGHT TO HELP BETTY!
WHAT?!
OH, ARCHIE! THAT'S SO SWEET OF YOU!!
OH, IT'S NOTHING AT ALL! RONNIE DOESN'T MIND! DO YOU, RONNIE?
OOOH, ARCHIE! HOLD ME TIGHT, I THINK I'M FALLING!!
...WELL, OF ALL THE NERVE !!
2

THAT SCHEMING LITTLE BLONDE! SHE PROBABLY CAN SKATE PRETTY GOOD!
I'LL SHOW HER, THAT WHEN IT COMES TO SCHEMING, SHE'S NO MATCH FOR VERONICA LODGE!!
ARCHIE, YOU'RE SO STRONG!
HOLD STEADY, BETTY! YOU'RE GETTING THE IDEA!.
WATCH THIS, ARCH!!... A JUMP REVERSE TURN!
OOPS!
THUMP!
BUMP!
3

ARE YOU ALL RIGHT, RONNIE?
OOWW! MY ANKLE!
I THINK I SPRAINED IT!!
LET'S GO OVER HERE AND SIT DOWN!
IS THERE MUCH PAIN?
I'M JUST A NATURAL SCHEMER!
ATTENTION SKATERS!! FIND YOURSELVES A PARTNER FOR THE DANCE NUMBER!

WOULD YOU DO ME THE HONOR OF BEING MY SKATE PARTNER, FOR THIS DANCE?
WOW!! WHAT A GOOD LOOKER!

WHY I'D BE DELIGHTED!
SHE WON'T BE ABLE TO!...SHE SPRAINED HER ANKLE!

I DID NO SUCH THING!! ... NOW IF YOU WILL EXCUSE ME!
?
... WHY DON'T YOU KIDS GO BRUSH UP ON YOUR PRACTICE?!
?!?!?
I'D SKATE WITH THIS DOLL EVEN WITH TWO SPRAINED ANKLES!
OH, HANK!
DEBBIE!! SO YOU DID MAKE IT AFTER ALL!!
!?
IT'S MY FIANCÉE! AND JUST IN TIME FOR THE DANCE NUMBER!
I GUESS IT'S JUST ONE OF THOSE DAYS!!
The END